IN THE COMPANY
OF CLOWNS

IN THE COMPANY
OF CLOWNS

A Commedia

by

MARTHA BACON

An Atlantic Monthly Press Book

LITTLE, BROWN AND COMPANY

BOSTON   TORONTO

Second Printing

T 04/73

Library of Congress Cataloging in Publication Data

Bacon, Martha Sherman
  In the company of clowns.

  SUMMARY: An orphan raised in a convent sees a new side of life while pursuing his donkey and a company of actors in eighteenth-century Italy.
  "An Atlantic Monthly Press book."
  [1. Italy--History--18th century--Fiction]
I. Title.
PZ7.B1345In   [Fic]   72-12893
ISBN 0-316-07510-8

ATLANTIC—LITTLE, BROWN BOOKS
ARE PUBLISHED BY
LITTLE, BROWN AND COMPANY
IN ASSOCIATION WITH
THE ATLANTIC MONTHLY PRESS

Published simultaneously in Canada
by Little, Brown & Company (Canada) Limited

PRINTED IN THE UNITED STATES OF AMERICA

For Alysoun, Antonia and Christopher

☙ ONE ☙

THERE IS real good in Gian-Piero," said Mother Matilda of the Convent of the Poor Clares to Sister Virgilia, her sacrist. Gian-Piero was within earshot and his heart sank at these fatal words and sank even further at Sister Virgilia's reply.

"Very true, Reverend Mother. He is diligent and humble — and he can read. It's a pity that he mayn't be a priest. No fault of his, poor child, that nobody knows who he is. Still he can become a clerk, there is plenty of room for clerks."

"It's a little early," remarked Mother Matilda, "to observe any signs of a vocation."

"A year or two should tell," replied the sacrist. "Thirteen or so usually decides these things. And he already serves very neatly at the altar."

"I wish he did not smell so strongly of the stables," said Mother Matilda. "Still, at bottom he is very good."

Gian-Piero's blood ran cold. His imagination surged ahead fifty — seventy-five years. He saw himself a crooked, snuffling cleric, knees callused from excessive prayers all unanswered, hobbling about the village of Rocca San Filippo, harassed by the cruel village children and laying his bones at last in the

graveyard behind the church, never having seen anything —
anything at all.

Gian-Piero — he had no other name — was an orphan and
an object of universal charity. As far as he knew he had come
into the world about ten years earlier without benefit of either
parent. He was beholden to Don Giugliano Basile, the parish
priest, for his clothing and he had spent the first years of his
life in Don Giugliano's kitchen cared for by Don Giugliano's
housekeeper, old Celestina. Don Giugliano had gained a considerable reputation for charity when he took in the orphan,
whom he said he found abandoned one evening in the confessional booth. The reputation flourished when Don Giugliano saw to it that the child was provided with food and
clothing and in winter even shoes. Orphans were not supposed to subsist in idleness for years on end, however, and
Gian-Piero had learned at an early age to make himself useful
around the village. The villagers, being very charitable people
and with the noble example of their priest before their eyes,
had managed to wrest from Gian-Piero a remarkable amount
of assorted labor in return for scraps of food and cast-off
clothing, a place by the fire on a cold evening, or, if the hearth
was too crowded, a corner of the stables. It was a fact that
Gian-Piero ate a lot, as much as you would give him, and then
he would like as not go begging for more next door. But as
Don Giugliano often said, boys *do* eat a lot. It was a comfort-
ing thought, true as the answers to the catechism or that other
fact — that he grew. "Boys *do* grow," said Don Giugliano,
and then someone in a spasm of generosity would give the boy
an old coat or a pair of ragged pantaloons.

Somehow Gian-Piero was fed and clad. Somehow he had

4

been baptized and he had learned to read. Don Giugliano had taught him.

Don Giugliano was lazy, disappointed and asthmatic, but he had not always been so. Once long ago he had entered the seminary full of bright ideas. He was the nephew of a provincial bishop and had thought of himself as occupying an exalted station in society. In Rome it had seemed less exalted than in Rocca where he came from. Nobody in Rome knew who his uncle was or cared to learn. He had loved knowledge or thought he had, until he found out that a little learning requires a great deal of work. Don Giugliano hated work much more than he loved learning. They taught him enough at the seminary to make a parish priest of him and to show him how little he really knew. He went back to Rocca chattering of the great sights he had seen while a student in Rome, mentioning the names of famous people and complaining that all preferment went to the illegitimate sons of cardinals. He whiled away the hours that fell between the sloppy performances of his priestly duties with picking out tunes on a mandolin to which he sang sweetly enough, reading French romances — he was addicted to them — and fondling his cats. He had five and was always getting more. Celestina howled around the parsonage that they left hairs on everything, were far from housebroken and had the evil eye. Because she was deaf and unemployable except as a priest's housekeeper, she and the cats remained.

Don Giugliano had merely added to her troubles when he had brought home six-week-old Gian-Piero in swaddling bands. "A work of charity for you," he said, handing her the child. "It will procure you much grace." Celestina felt that

5

the cats should be procuring her all the grace she needed. Were they not, after all, the cats of a bishop's nephew? She grumbled but she took the child since she couldn't very well drop him and she raised him on goat's milk — the parsonage kept two goats and a donkey — and later on bread and garlic and olive oil and he throve.

Don Giugliano paid little attention to Gian-Piero, who grew into a pretty dark-haired boy with large gray eyes and who gave very little trouble even by Celestina's standards. He seemed to know that sickness or getting into mischief would prove the end of him so he stayed healthy and did not turn wicked. When he was five years old, Don Giugliano taught him to read out of his breviary. Gian-Piero learned quickly and when he had read through the breviary and got the answers to the catechism by heart, Don Giugliano brought him before his uncle, the bishop, to be confirmed. That was in the year 1710. Then Don Giugliano turned his attention to the mandolin, the French novels and the cats and bothered him no more.

Gian-Piero picked grapes, shoveled manure, stirred the vats full of blue copper dust with which to spray the crops against pests, ran errands for the apothecary, herded and milked goats, ground maize and served at the altar on Sundays and feast days. Then one day Mother Matilda of the Convent of the Poor Clares, which stood just outside the village, went looking for a scullion. Gian-Piero happened to come into view on his way to the apothecary's shop and she took his appearance for a sign. From then on Gian-Piero had permanent employment scrubbing pots and pans for Sister Agnese, the cellaress, and serving at the nuns' altar when not required in the kitchen.

If anyone had asked him what he thought of his life, which nobody ever did, he would have replied that there was nothing really wrong with it. He was not blind like the apothecary's son, nor harelipped like Sebastiano Morello, the cobbler, nor half-witted like Alessandra Bevilaqua's poor Stefano, but his life lacked color. Somewhere beyond the jagged marble peaks which reared up behind the poor little village, almost pushing it into the sea, the illegitimate sons of cardinals wore red clothes and feasted on guinea fowl and candied chestnuts. People danced. Beautiful marchesas with red hair were ferried in gondolas to masked balls in Venice. Dukes trod stately minuets by moonlight in Florence. The Pope jigged in the Vatican and even poodles performed gavottes to the sound of fiddles in city squares which were lit up all night for the pleasure of the spectators. He had read of these things in Don Giugliano's books. For Gian-Piero there was no dancing. They were going to make a friar of him.

He saw no avenues of escape. Nobody was going to give him the ruined castle which stood on the cliff above the town, the dark tower which had once, long ago guarded the town against the assaults of Levantine pirates. It would make a fine house if properly repaired, and Gian-Piero occasionally fancied himself lord of it, free to pace its windy battlements and commander of the waves which broke at its foundations. In his daydreams he called it *his* tower. It was a fine piece of property and gave him much pleasure but made him no richer.

7

He had even considered marriage. The Baronessa Corvo, who lived in the Palazzo Corvo a half mile from the village, had a granddaughter of seventeen, the young Baronessa Ermina Corvo. She was a thin girl with crooked teeth and narrow eyes set so closely that they seemed yearning to meet at the bridge of her nose. In the village it was said that her looks were no problem since her fortune would secure her almost any husband that she set her mind to.

Gian-Piero had taken the opportunity of inspecting her on one occasion when he delivered a load of kindling to the Palazzo. He had gazed at her fixedly for some minutes from under a bundle of faggots which almost totally hid him from her. She did not see him at all mainly because she had eyes for nobody but a certain Contino di Carcaci who was a pallid young man of twenty, and already showing signs of the many chins he would own in later life.

Even if the Baronessa Ermina could have been persuaded to overlook the difference in their ages — about seven years — Gian-Piero did not quite see how he could ever recommend himself to a wife who was apparently so charmed by so much pale bulk encased in green velvet and white satin, by so many smiles and compliments and flourishing bows. And besides, the villagers said that the Contino was also enormously rich. Money loves money. How did a poor boy get a rich wife? It was a common enough occurrence and one heard of its happening every day but nobody ever explained how it was done. Watching this unwholesome young couple, Gian-Piero developed an unconquerable aversion to a woman who could fancy anything so plump and white and pouting as the Contino. A rich wife with large eyes and curls, drawn to stormy,

8

slender boys, was what Gian-Piero needed but there was no-body of that description in Rocca.

And here it was Easter Monday and he was scouring pots in the courtyard of the kitchen of the Poor Clares. Sister Agnese, who was busy picking over a bowl full of snails called from the kitchen for her big iron kettle. He heaved it up and brought it to her. She peered at it with nearsighted eyes as though she were trying to make up her mind what it was. She finally made it out and did not like it. She handed the pot back to Gian-Piero, at the same time delivering a box on his ear which set lightning flashing before his eyes.

"Is that what you call a scrubbed pot? It's filthy. You expect me to cook for the sisters in that?"

"It's perfectly clean, Sister," he urged. "Not a spot on it."

"I tell you it's black with grease."

"Feel it," he begged. She was so blind that she continuously saw what wasn't there. She grudgingly ran a finger around the inner rim of the kettle. It was smooth and clean enough and with a grunt of discontent she turned back into the kitchen, knocking her nose against the doorjamb as she went. Gian-Piero took some satisfaction in seeing that she struck herself quite a blow, as was only just, and it served him for an apology. His ears were ringing from the clout she had given him and he realized as the kitchen door slammed behind the old nun that she was not going to give him anything to eat. Tears welled in his eyes. He stood in the courtyard, the evening breeze plucking at his thin clothes and his stomach snarling with hunger. The convent bell rang for vespers. There wouldn't be a mouthful until after compline. He should be serving at the altar now but he was too hungry and

9

disappointed to make the effort. He began to concoct a plausible story to account for his absence, a lie with enough truth in it to enforce belief.

Gian-Piero dealt expertly in lies. He had been manufacturing them from an early age, believable confections which when explored were so complicated that they could scarcely be classified as falsehoods. It wasn't that they contradicted the facts involved; they merely had little to do with them. But experience had taught him that a grain of truth added flavor to the inventions so he always tried to include one.

It was these fabrications of Gian-Piero's which convinced Mother Matilda of his essential goodness. She would point admiringly to all those aspects of his lies which corresponded with the facts and praise Gian-Piero's diligence, humility and poverty. She talked of his poverty as though it were a virtue which he had carefully cultivated in spite of the opportunities for riches besetting him on all sides.

Gian-Piero clopped across the scullery yard. Heavy wooden-soled shoes made him walk slowly. He picked his way through the greening fennel stalks in the vegetable garden and pushed open the door of the stable. From the depths of one of the two stalls a pair of eyes gleamed at him. They belonged to an old friend, a donkey called Domenico.

"Out, Domenico, out!" He caught the donkey by the halter and led it into the courtyard. A slap on Domenico's rump sent the donkey trotting across the vegetable plot and out the gate into the road.

"Domenico's loose," shouted Gian-Piero. "Help! Domenico's got loose again."

Domenico quickened his pace since this was what was

wanted of him and Gian-Piero set off after him, keeping a short distance between himself and the donkey and squalling for assistance from time to time when anyone came into view. "I've got to catch Domenico. Someone help me catch Domenico. Tell Mother Matilda that Domenico's loose and I am running after him."

By the time he and Domenico had reached the church in the middle of the village Gian-Piero had a sizable collection of witnesses to his story.

Domenico stopped by the well and began to crop at the few mouthfuls of weeds that straggled around its base and Gian-Piero made a great show of creeping up to him and seizing his halter. Domenico laid back his ears, brayed and kicked at the cobblestones. Gian-Piero stroked his neck as a reward for a job well done and glanced slyly around to see if anyone was noticing. Nobody was. They were all watching something else. Never in all his life had Gian-Piero seen the square so busy.

Two or three dozen people were setting up a kind of scaffold on the church steps and Gian-Piero's first thought was that an execution of more than ordinary importance was about to take place, but as he watched the progress of the scaffolding and the behavior of the builders he decided that they were not going to hang or behead anybody. There was no gallows nor was there a block nor an ax. Instead there was a fine crimson curtain edged with gold fringe which was strung on ropes in front of the platform. Several people were running it back and forth to make sure that it opened and closed smoothly. A bench in front of the curtain was serving as a kind of minor stage for a man who walked on his hands.

11

A dog, all snowy curls and pompons and wearing a gold collar studded with bits of glass, jumped on the bench and danced across it on his hind legs. The man caught him at the end of the bench, tossed him a sweet and made him a deep bow. The dog snapped the sweet and bowed in his turn. Snatches of music trickled through the shouts of the carpenters setting up the scaffold, the cries of the acrobats and the incessant barking of the dog. Gian-Piero, with Domenico's halter in his hand, stared at all of this with his mouth wide open and his toes turned in and wondered if, on this Easter Monday of all Easter Mondays, his luck had changed.

"Well, my fine fellow! And have you come to see the show?"

He felt a heavy hand on his shoulder and turned to look up into the face of a tall, fat man wearing a stupendous smile.

The smile was not the only notable thing he was wearing. He sported a wig of gleaming white horsehair under a round black hat. A red satin waistcoat was buttoned over his generous paunch. His breeches were also of red satin and Gian-Piero had never seen such a pair of pantaloons. Over all of this he wore what seemed to be a dressing gown of black velvet and his feet were shod in black velvet slippers with long toes that curled up.

"My donkey ran away," said Gian-Piero. "I was chasing my donkey."

"It's the way of donkeys," said the man. "That's a very fine donkey. What would you take for him?"

"I don't think he's for sale," said Gian-Piero.

12

"Ah, but what if I gave you — let me see now — what if I gave you twelve scudi and let you see the show free."

"Twelve scudi!" gasped Gian-Piero. He had scarcely realized there was that much money in the world. With that kind of capital a rich wife was no longer a necessity. "What's the show?" he asked.

"Any one of half a dozen," said the man comfortably. "What do you say to *The Queen of England and Milord Essex?* It's a fine comedy and they execute milord. Or there's *The Cursing of the Old Man in Love.* I play the old man."

"Why do you want my donkey?" asked Gian-Piero.

"My donkey died last night." The man swept a white silk handkerchief from his pocket and dabbed at the corner of his left eye. "He died of a surfeit. He'd been with me, man and boy, these thirty years and then he keeled over and died without a word of warning, right in the middle of my scene with the Doctor from Bologna."

"You mean your donkey was an actor?"

"The best," said the man. "He's a dreadful loss to the theatre."

"Domenico can't act," said Gian-Piero.

"Domenico? Oh, your donkey — the one you're going to sell me. Don't disturb yourself. He'll learn easily enough. Look at that dog there. I taught him to dance. I'll make a comedian of Domenico by tomorrow evening. Think of the life he'll have. The sound of applause, beautiful women, riches. And think of the twelve scudi. You know, you look hungry. What do you say we go to dinner? They have good sausage in the tavern. I know, I saw them making it this morning. Some sausage and a bit of eggplant and some

14

ricotta and a couple of eggs, a bottle of wine and an almond tart."

Gian-Piero cast a desperate look at Domenico and then secured him by the rope on his halter to a stanchion near the well where, ignorant of the splendid fate in store for him, he continued to crop weeds. Then with a sigh Gian-Piero followed his new business acquaintance into the tavern.

🕮 TWO 🕮

Now, SIR," said the fat man, "what will you have to eat? Suit yourself. Money's no object and the landlord serves everything."

Gian-Piero, blinking in the greenish light of the tavern and half fainting at the inspiring smells drifting from the kitchen, merely opened his mouth and blinked.

The fat man chattered on in a lazy and slightly squeaky voice which sounded like a door moving on hinges which wanted oiling. "Bring the boy some wine, landlord. When he's drunk a little he'll know better what he wants. Bring us some of your best wine."

The landlord's best wine was dark red and raw and it went down Gian-Piero's gullet and coiled itself like a warm snake at the pit of his stomach. The warmth made him feel powerful and when the landlord came around again he ordered like a sultan. He attacked the meal with real savagery, as though the pigeon pie and boiled fennel and sausages and tarts would escape him. He realized that the ponderous actor and the landlord thought his appetite very funny. Over the noise of the tavern their uproarious laughter thundered in his ears. He laughed with them and drank his wine. He had never seen such a pair of good fellows in his life.

16

There was a great deal of talk. The fat man gave a speech about love and art, two subjects which did not interest Gian-Piero. The speech was interrupted by frequent applause and the fat man became more eloquent as more people crowded into the room. The tavern began to swirl around Gian-Piero and he discovered to his amusement that his fat friend had two heads. He shut one eye and tapped the side of his nose but the fat man continued to add heads. Gian-Piero closed both eyes. His own head, which had suddenly become too heavy for his shoulders, dropped toward the table. He felt the tavern rising and falling under him like a ship in a storm. It rocked him to sleep and then rocked him awake again. The fat man had dropped art and love and was discoursing on money. The landlord was talking about it too, very angrily, along with a group of other people in brightly colored clothes. Some of them were wearing masks. The conversation had become a quarrel. The landlord was shouting and so was the fat man, abetted by his fancy friends. A bottle sailed through the air and smashed against the wall. Gian-Piero stared, hypnotized at the expensive trickle of red wine against the rough-cast wall of the tavern. Other missiles followed the bottle. A plate whistled by one ear and a candlestick smashed against the wall behind him. Gian-Piero slipped from his chair and found peace under the table where, hidden by the cloth, he curled up and fell asleep again.

He awoke in a cold stale hush. Pulling the tablecloth aside he saw a spring morning shining outside the tavern grille. Gian-Piero crawled out on his hands and knees and struggled to his feet, trying to remember why he was here. The room looked totally unfamiliar. It had been packed with people

17

last night and had seemed small and cozy. Now it looked large and empty and Gian-Piero, who had been warm and happy and well fed, was as cold and lonely as ever. And in addition he felt sick. Too much sausage and almond tart, he thought. He was not used to such food. The diet at the Poor Clares did not include any of the delicacies he had eaten last night. Even in his desolate condition he thought affectionately of that pigeon pie with strips of ham and currants in it. He also began to remember why he was here. It was all because of Domenico. He had agreed to sell Domenico to the fat man who was going to make an actor of him.

Gian-Piero gave himself a shake. The fat man had promised him twelve scudi but no amount of shaking caused the sound of jingling coinage. A number of uncomfortable thoughts slid into his mind. He had been cheated, robbed. And, moreover, Domenico was not his donkey to sell. How was he to return to Mother Matilda with neither Domenico nor any money to show for him? He would have to make up one of his lies; he and Domenico had been waylaid by brigands. Domenico had run away to become an actor. Mother Matilda would swallow a lot but both of these tales were likely to stick in even her craw. Besides, the tavern had been full of people who would remember that Gian-Piero had spent the evening there. He would have to recover Domenico and then find a story to account for his absence.

Gian-Piero lifted the latch of the tavern door and peeked out into the square. The early sun splashed light on the white stone church and flickered in the central fountain. The square was very quiet, so quiet that Gian-Piero could hear the lapping of waves against the docks where the village met the sea and the crowing of a cock in a nearby chicken roost. There was no sign of Domenico and the stage had been removed. The players had evidently left town. Turning back into the tavern Gian-Piero saw the landlord, sleepy-eyed, stumbling into the taproom to pour himself a measure of spirits.

"The fat man, where is he?" exclaimed Gian-Piero.

"Fat man!" The landlord took a gulp of brandy and also a bite from the heel of a loaf which he held in his hand. "Which fat man?"

"The fat man in the funny clothes. The player. He owes me twelve scudi."

"Owes you —" The landlord broke into a howl of laughter. "And me — what do you think he owes me? And for your dinner too. So what are you planning to do? Hire a lawyer. No. You can give me a day's work for your dinner and think yourself lucky to have eaten it."

"But he's got my donkey," wailed Gian-Piero. "Where's he gone to?"

"What do you mean your donkey? You don't own any donkey."

"I mean Mother Matilda's donkey," said Gian-Piero. "I left him tied up by the well. He's gone. I have to find him." He decided to suppress the problem of the debt of twelve scudi. Someone would be bound to hold it against him that he was trying to collect for Mother Matilda's Domenico.

"Well, you can't," said the landlord. "The whole troupe went last night, as soon as the show was over. So much the worse for you if they stole your donkey. I suppose he wasn't

19

nailed down. You'll learn better than to trust a gaggle of comedians next time. And so will I."

"But where did they go?"

"How should I know? To Venice, I guess."

"Is Venice very far?"

"Far enough. Cheating and pulling teeth on the way."

"Pulling teeth?"

"One of them — the fellow who plays the Doctor from Bologna — is a dentist on the side. I should have had a tooth pulled for the price of one of those dinners. It's a sad waste that I don't have a toothache. You can get busy and help me clean up and think on the lesson you've learned. Actors! They talk about love and art. Money is nothing in the minds of such great folk as they, but somebody pays for the dinners and clears away the mess. That's where love and art get you. The free life! I'm a soulless man of business, that's what I am. Those angels in satin cloaks and hats with peacock feathers are crawling with lice just like any other beggar if you ask me. Well, now you see what comes of running after vagabonds who can't settle to an honest living. Love everyone like a brother until it comes time to pay up. Love! Art!" The landlord's feelings overwhelmed him and he spat disgustedly on the floor. "Well, the sooner you and I forget about love and art the sooner we'll get this place to rights."

"But Mother Matilda's donkey —" said Gian-Piero.

"Oh, he's gone for good," said the landlord. "How did he happen to be in the village anyway?"

"He got out of his stall."

"Someone must have been very careless," said the landlord pointedly. "You've lost him but that's water under the bridge

20

now. Take these glasses to the pump and wash them. There's no use moping over the donkey. Wishing won't bring him back."

Gian-Piero eyed the landlord and then the door. The landlord was stout. He would hardly have wind for a chase if Gian-Piero bolted. He scuttled across the room, darted through the door and slammed it behind him. In the square he paused for a moment to consider which direction to take for Venice. The Carrara Mountains reared up behind him; the Tyrrhenian Sea lay in front. He slipped into an alley. Somewhere behind him he heard the heavy tread of someone in pursuit. The landlord, probably, not to be plundered of a day's work. Gian-Piero slipped down the alley and along the wall which stood between the church and the street. A door in the wall led into the cloister behind the church. Gian-Piero knew the cloister well. He had spent the first five years of his life in it. The cloister, almost a ruin now, gave easy access to the church. Gian-Piero could hide there until the landlord had reconciled himself to the loss of a scullion. Then he could make a plan for the recovery of Domenico.

The door was just ahead of him. He passed through it, crossed the cloister and entered the church behind the altar. The church was empty. The sun shone through the high arched windows, picked out the stations of the cross and touched the image of the Holy Mother, who with outstretched arms looked down on a few votive candles and a cluster of dandelions in a glass. Someone had already been there with a petition. Gian-Piero caught up a taper and lit another votive candle with an urgent request for the swift return of Domenico. He was murmuring an earnest if hasty Ave Maria when his ear caught a curious and unmistakable sound. Some-one had sneezed. He looked enquiringly at the Holy Mother. She had been known to weep, he knew, but he had never heard that she had sneezed. Her sweet blue-eyed gaze appeared to be bent upon him but she was quite motionless. Gian-Piero's eyes slid around the church.

"*Gratia plena* —." Another sneeze. "*Et benedictus fructus ventris tui, Jesu.*" A third sneeze. It was certainly not Our Lady. It was a man's sneeze. Gian-Piero moved cautiously up the aisle to where the rood screen intervened between the main body of the church and the altar and peered through the black and gold grille. He found himself gazing into a pair of eyes.

The eyes met his unswervingly — a keen, searching look. The eyes, narrow, almond-shaped and dark were set in a youngish, lantern-jawed face which was pale and shadowed by a day-old beard.

"Did you sneeze?" asked Gian-Piero.

"Yes, I'm catching a cold. It's drafty in here."

"Why don't you come out then?"

"I can't."

"Why not?"

"I've taken sanctuary."

"Sanctuary from what?"

"My debts. The innkeeper is after me. He wants blood from a turnip. What can I do? I can't give him back his dinner. I've eaten it."

"Are you one of the players?"

The stranger smiled, gave himself a shake and came out

from behind the rood screen. He was a tall, lanky young man, loose-limbed and supple as a snake. Standing there in the church with his large slender hands dangling limply from his wrists, his shoulders sagging and his knees slightly bent, he reminded Gian-Piero of a marionette. His dark eyes were extremely bright, glittering as a reptile's eyes, and his complexion was sallow. He had a cold in his pear-shaped nose. He was dressed in a patchwork suit of rousing shades of red, green and yellow diamonds. One slender leg wore a black stocking and the other one was encased in yellow. A white frill surrounded his throat like the petals of a flower. A black mask with a long black nose was perched jauntily on his head instead of a cap.

"Harlequin at your service," he said and bowed. "Cousin to the devil. And who may you be?"

"I'm Gian-Piero. I'm a foundling. Where are all the other players gone?"

"Gone!" said the actor. "What do you mean — gone?"

"They've left. They went off in the night and took my donkey with them."

"In that case," said Harlequin, "they will have gone toward Lucca. And I take it very badly that they left me behind to pay the score. However, it's no great matter. I shall catch up with them and slip a raw egg down Pantaloon's neck."

"Is Pantaloon a big fat man in satin trousers?"

"That would describe him."

"He has my donkey. He must give me back my donkey."

"If he has your donkey that is easier said than done. Pantaloon never gave anybody anything."

23

"It's not even my donkey. He belongs to Mother Matilda."

"That makes matters worse," said Harlequin.

"Will you help me get him back?"

"I can take you to where he is."

"Are you really cousin to the devil?"

"So some people say."

"Is Harlequin your real name?"

"No."

"What is it then?"

"Leonardo da Vinci."

Gian-Piero snorted. "He invented a flying machine. And he's dead besides. You are not Leonardo da Vinci."

"I see that you are a very bright boy. How did you know that Leonardo da Vinci was dead?"

"I read it in a book."

"Ah, books now. Are you in the habit of reading books?"

"Not exactly. I only read them sometimes."

"It's unusual to meet a boy who reads books. Most healthy wholesome boys — boys like me — avoid them. Tell me. Can you read anything, anything at all?"

"Yes, I think so. So long as it's in a language I know."

"Can you read that?" asked Harlequin. He pointed to a stone plaque in the wall with letters picked out in gold leaf.

Gian-Piero peered at it. The writing was a little obscured because some of the gold leaf had worn off, but it was legible.

"Here lies — Sebastiano Mancini — for forty years — priest of this parish — a faithful guardian of the flock —"

"That is quite right," said Harlequin, gazing at the plaque. "I could use a bright boy who can read. Would you like to read stories for me?"

"I suppose so," said Gian-Piero, "but I can't stop to read now. I have to find Domenico and bring him back to Mother Matilda."

"I shall strike a bargain with you," said Harlequin. "If I help you to find your donkey will you read a few tales for me? You might even write them down for me. I require new ideas at frequent intervals."

The bargain did not sound a bad one. Gian-Piero said, "Yes, if it doesn't take too long. I'll get a beating if I come back without the donkey."

"Why come back?"

"But I have to. I live here."

"But you're a foundling. You have no father or mother. Why not travel and see the world?"

"But what will the Poor Clares do without a donkey?"

"God will send them a donkey. A bright boy like you shouldn't spend his life begging his way around a convent. Why, who knows, if you come to Venice you might find your father."

"My *father!*"

"Well, you must have had one. Perhaps he's a great count or marchese who will take you to his bosom. 'Ah, my long-lost son! Who would have believed it? Have you black hair and gray eyes? Yes, you have. Then you must be he.' He'll leave you a fortune when he dies."

"Now I know you must be cousin to the devil," said Gian-Piero. "You are trying to tempt me. Anyway, why should he be in Venice?"

"Because that's where all the money is. Anything can happen in Venice. And besides, think of the donkey," said Harlequin. "He is probably crying his eyes out for you this very moment."

"No, he isn't," said Gian-Piero. "He doesn't even like me very much."

"Well, he won't like Pantaloon any better. Pantaloon will beat and starve him. That's how the other donkey died."

"He said the donkey was an actor. I must find poor Domenico."

The devil's cousin was very tempting. In Rocca Gian-Piero would have to grow up to be a cleric. Perhaps this was his chance to escape. Suppose that he went with this Harlequin. What had he to lose? If he was not happy he could always take Domenico and run back to Rocca with a ready-made story which could only do him credit. He could bring the donkey back in triumph to the Poor Clares after having risked life and limb to restore him to his rightful owners.

He turned to confront Harlequin and saw him walking up and down in front of the Holy Mother — on his hands. The actor did a sudden flip, turned a somersault in midair and landed on his feet.

"Come," said Harlequin briskly. "Let us be off before they think to look for us here."

"Won't they recognize you if you step out in those clothes?" said Gian-Piero. "They'll see you and catch you and put you in jail."

"A bright boy like you thinks of everything," said Harlequin. "Perhaps you'd better find me a disguise."

"I don't see how I can do that."

"All I need is a dark cloak. Where does the priest keep his cloak?"

26

"In his house, of course."

"Then steal it for me."

"But I can't. He'd catch me."

"If you don't steal the priest's cloak for me I shall cut your throat."

"You wouldn't!" gasped Gian-Piero. Harlequin thrust his hand to his side and pulled a short but extremely sharp knife from his belt. He flicked it under Gian-Piero's nose. "See that. It will find you out. Feel it." He laid the flat of the knife against Gian-Piero's cheek. "Feel how cold it is. I took it from a friend who refused me a favor. He's dead. Get me the priest's cloak and you'll live to be a hundred. Don't get it —" The knife flashed again just under Gian-Piero's nose.

"I shall get it, Signore." Gian-Piero ducked behind the altar, into the cloister and from there crossed the alley which led into Don Giugliano's kitchen. His heart boomed against his ribs. It did not occur to him to bolt from the devil's cousin. Those dark snake-eyes would find him out.

He stood for a moment quaking in the kitchen, aware that Celestina was stirring in her own bedroom and would intercept him at any moment. Don Giugliano's cloak, a cassock and his biretta hung from a set of pegs on the wall beside the fireplace. Gian-Piero snatched them all and streaked out the kitchen door, stumbling over one of the cats who took advantage of the open door to whip into the kitchen. The cat distracted Celestina's attention. He heard her remonstrating with it as he scuttled into the church and flung the clothes at Harlequin. "There, take them and be off."

The actor slipped the cassock over his shoulders, folded

himself into the cloak, doffed the mask, put on the biretta and said, "Are you ready, my son?"

"Ready?"

"Ready to shake the dust of this place from your sandals."

"No. You go. I don't want to."

"And leave you to set the constables on me the moment my back is turned? Besides, how will you explain to the priest about his cloak? It was your idea that I should be disguised, you know. How will you restore the donkey to the nuns?"

"I don't know." Gian-Piero looked wildly around the church. He was trapped. He could neither go nor stay. He had disposed of enough ecclesiastical property to hang half a dozen foundlings, he supposed. He turned in supplication to the Holy Mother. She was smiling.

Harlequin turned, genuflected to the altar and then raised his hand in benediction. "Come, my son. Let us be on our way. *Pax vobiscum.*"

✿ THREE ✿

A WELL-MUFFLED PRIEST and a ragged small boy were not a spectacle to excite notice along the mountain roads beyond Rocca San Filippo. Once an old woman carrying a load of firewood stopped them and asked for a blessing which Harlequin dispensed in so sweet a voice and with such a winning smile that when she got home she declared that she had encountered an angel and led a virtuous life for several days afterwards.

About noon Harlequin cast himself before a roadside shrine and prayed fervently for a meal. Gian-Piero prayed too but without faith. There was no sign of food anywhere. The budding vines had as yet no fruit to offer and the fruit trees were all in flower. However they did discover a goat nibbling at the new grass in a lonely pasture. It was a nanny goat and she was tethered casually to a tree on a long rope. Where there is a nanny goat there is likely to be a pail, and a few minutes' search yielded one, hidden in a thicket under a chestnut tree. Harlequin milked the goat and he and Gian-Piero shared a generous amount of goat's milk which Harlequin measured out with great precision, allowing a slight edge in Gian-Piero's favor. He then rinsed the pail in a nearby stream and put it back where he had found it under the chestnut tree and the two travelers trudged on their way.

"If the troupe is making for Venice — which it is," said Harlequin, "there is only one direction to follow — northeast. To go southwest would be folly, even possibly blasphemy."

"Is it much farther?" asked Gian-Piero.

"Is what much farther?"

"Venice."

"A step or two, my son. Kindly remember to say Father when you speak to me."

"Yes, Father. But you're not a priest."

"Ah, my son, that is the interesting part of the story."

Gian-Piero glanced at his companion. It crept into his mind that Harlequin was mad. Madmen fancied that they were the Pope or even the Lord Himself. Harlequin's features wore an expression of sweet serenity that well became a priest or a madman. The mountain wind wound the dark cloak around his agile body and plucked at the mask which he had smoothed down under the collar. The mask leered at Gian-Piero like a second face and Harlequin smoothed it under his chin and flashed a third face at the boy, a grinning clown who closed one eye and thrust his tongue into his cheek. The clown vanished, the eyelids drooped and the mouth drew down in a pious grimace. How many masks were there, wondered Gian-Piero. And if one stripped them all away what lay beneath the final mask? The thought made his flesh crawl and he shivered.

"Are you cold, my son?"

"Yes."

"I shall carry you a little way under my cloak."

He swooped Gian-Piero up in his arms, folded the cloak, which was ample, around Gian-Piero and nestled him in his arms.

"Thank you, Father," said Gian-Piero desperately.

"We must find a village, my son," said Harlequin.

"That we must," said Gian-Piero.

"Don't you know the villages in this neighborhood?" asked Harlequin. "Surely a boy born and bred here —"

"I've been to Poveromo," said Gian-Piero, "but I've never gone into the hills before. I always stayed in Rocca."

"We must pray for a village," said Harlequin. "Pray."

"Yes, Father."

Evening was coming on, and the wind, fierce as a bandit, knifed down from the Appennines.

"Or even a haystack," said Harlequin.

"Holy Mother, send us a haystack," prayed Gian-Piero.

In the gathering dusk the countryside huddled against the dangers of the dark like a scared animal. Gian-Piero clung to his strange protector, puzzled as to whether to be more frightened of him or of the night. Peeping out from the folds of the cloak he could see the stars but no other light. In the dark every wicked thing which hid itself by day took a vague but visible shape. Evil was everywhere, perhaps most of all in this imp disguised as a priest who cradled Gian-Piero close and butted his head against the wind like a ram against a barn door.

"Harlequin isn't your real name, is it?" asked Gian-Piero. "Harlequin isn't a real person," he added.

"Certainly he is," replied the actor.

"Are you baptized?"

"Of course. Do you take me for one of the damned?"

"You said you were the devil's cousin."

"A man isn't judged by his relatives, otherwise what would be the use of good works? My name is Agostino Molino. I come of a long line of priests. The part comes naturally to me."

From the hills came a long chilling sound, the unmistakable howl of a wolf. "The Mother of Rome calling to her whelps," whispered Agostino. He quickened his pace, almost to a run. Then he stopped. Gian-Piero felt him draw a long breath. "I see a light," he said. "I think we are coming to a farmhouse."

This proved to be the case. Harlequin put Gian-Piero on his feet and a few more paces brought them to within a few yards of a cluster of buildings, a barn, a hen roost, a pigsty and a farmhouse. Harlequin smoothed the cloak about him, settled the biretta firmly on his head and approached the cottage door where a low light burned in an adjoining window. His knock was speedily answered. A woman opened the door.

She was a broad, hearty woman and when she saw the priest in the doorway she broke into a wide smile.

"Father! Come in. We thought you'd never arrive."

For a moment Harlequin seemed to lose his poise. His jaw dropped an instant but his recovery was rapid. "Bless you, my daughter," he said and crossed the threshold into a clean warm kitchen.

"I've been watching for you this half hour," said the woman. "You've no notion of what it is to be without a priest. Poor old Father Girolamo! He will be so relieved. I must run to the village and tell him you've got here. You'll want to hear the confessions at once, won't you? Well, the church isn't far, a ten-minute trot. Let me give you a glass of wine and then there's time enough to hear their sins."

"How long is it since they have confessed themselves?" enquired Harlequin.

"Let me see now . . . poor Father Girolamo has been laid up with the lumbago since ten days after Candlemas. Things have gone to rack and ruin in the parish. We haven't had a Mass said here for six weeks and more. Well, that's all over now. We shall have a Mass tomorrow morning."

"You live a lonely life here," said Harlequin casually.

"You're right, Father. Not many visitors come our way. No opera house here."

"The commedia troupe didn't visit you, I suppose."

"Passed this way this morning but stopped only for breakfast. Left without paying the bill at the tavern as like as not." The signora had no truck with comedians. A fine immoral lot they were. The men and women hardly ever bothered to marry but merely lived together producing little zanies. The medicines they sold on the side did no good. The signora knew; she had tried them all. They neither cured the toothache, curled the hair nor kept husbands faithful. She would have nothing to do with charlatans and mountebanks. As for the troupe which the Father had enquired about, she had not even seen them. She thought they might be making their way to Sant'Ursula, quite a distance ahead. But whichever way they went they were a thieving lot. Beppina the watchdog had fallen to barking

34

about dawn and now the good wife was missing two Leghorn pullets, so it all went to show that actors were not to be trusted.

"Correct, my daughter. They are worse than foxes."

"You sound as though you spoke from experience, Father." She poured more wine and then offered to escort the new priest to church. "We'll have supper when you're through with them, Father," she said, "and you can sleep at Father Girolamo's tonight. We'll put the boy in the barn. He'll be warm enough there."

"We dine after the confessions have been heard?" enquired Harlequin.

"Yes, to be sure," chuckled the signora. "And you're hungry I expect and so is the boy. I've a boiled chicken and some sausage. And there is a panforte."

"Very good. Bless you, my daughter." The blessing contained the remission of at least a hundred days in Purgatory, Gian-Piero thought. He hoped that there would not be many penitents.

Six weeks worth of sins took quite a while to confess but the dinner was worth waiting for and the new priest made himself extremely agreeable over it and over the bottle of red wine that went with it. The signora was delighted with the new cleric: a nice country boy. None of your fancy city priests who thought themselves above their parishioners, but a man of simple country virtues and a good appetite. He was what she liked to see in a priest and he took such good care of his nephew, insisting on taking him to the barn himself in order to see that he said his prayers before sleeping.

Harlequin heaped straw for Gian-Piero and whispered,

35

"Sleep now. I shall be back for you soon. It won't do to be taken alive," and caught up the lantern and disappeared, leaving Gian-Piero to watch and wonder in the darkness.

He wondered if Agostino Molino would say Mass in the morning and if so would he be struck by lightning? Somewhere he had heard that to masquerade as a priest was a very dangerous thing to do. He had half expected a stray lightning bolt to find its target during the confessional but nothing had happened and both the signora and Harlequin had returned from church quite content with his performance. It seemed that the Lord had overlooked the blasphemy but Gian-Piero had his doubts as to how much the saints would put up with. While he wondered in the warm straw, lulled by the gentle breathing of two cows and a calf, he fell asleep and was startled out of a dream almost immediately — or so it seemed — by a hand across his mouth and a whisper hissing in his ear.

"Out. It's the time to get out."

"Already? But what will they say in the morning when they find you gone? You promised to say Mass."

"Leave that to the other priest. He's bound to come along sooner or later. We must be gone when he comes or there'll be the devil to pay."

Gian-Piero struggled to his feet. Harlequin was holding the barn door open and already a faint streak of dawn was showing in the eastern sky. Even as they stole out of the barnyard the first cock began to crow and sent Harlequin streaking like a greased pig through the little hamlet with Gian-Piero stumbling in his clumsy shoes and clinging to Harlequin's cloak with both hands.

They had put the village well behind them before Agostino slackened his pace. Finally he paused, somewhat out of breath, beside a shrine of Saint Anthony of Padua and said, "Now we may have our breakfast."

He took from the folds of his cloak a leather bag which contained a very satisfactory breakfast. It not only included the remains of last night's dinner but several other dainties besides: a mozzarella cheese, a roasted rabbit, a bottle of wine, a loaf of bread and a honeycomb.

Again Harlequin offered Gian-Piero generous portions of everything and urged the wine on him as a tonic. "It will keep you warm for the rest of the journey," he said.

"How did you get the signora to give you all that?" asked Gian-Piero.

"Actually I did not consult her. I felt she would be happier not knowing."

"You mean you stole it all?"

"Borrowed, my son. And Christians are instructed to feed the hungry."

"They will be very angry when they come to Mass and find you are not there and all the food gone," said Gian-Piero.

"Precisely. They will say that they always knew that comedians were not to be trusted. Finish your wine. We must be on our way. It is urgent that we catch the troupe before they reach Lucca."

"Are you sure they've gone to Lucca? I thought they were going to Venice."

"Lucca first. Then Venice. One leads to another. Fortunately those confessions were not all for nothing though they were boring enough. People in small towns have so little to

37

confess and what they do confess is always the wrong thing. When one boasts of the sin of anger one can be fairly sure that it is sloth he is worried about. His anger came because someone disturbed him. It is seldom that one hears anyone confess to anything that he's really committed."

"Have you heard many confessions?" asked Gian-Piero.

"Never before," replied Harlequin, "but I know how *I* do it. Now with me gluttony is an excellent sin to confess to. I shall certainly confess to eating this cheese."

"But not to stealing it?"

"How can you accuse me of stealing it? You yourself heard the signora offer me everything the house afforded. However, I said there was one thing to be had from the confessions. I learned for a certainty that the rest of the troupe is on the Lucca road. One of the penitents told me so. She met with them early yesterday morning on the way back from the milking and stopped for some entertainment with Pantaloon. The disreputable old goat! I gave her a very stiff penance. And she a respectable married woman! It was in fact the only interesting confession of the lot. It was quite worth hearing. Pantaloon will be sorry."

He stood up and shook the crumbs from the cloak, spat on a finger and held it up to the wind. "It is going to rain. And me with a cold."

The rain came about a half an hour later. It began with a few scattered drops and built to a steady downpour accompanied by a sharp wind from the mountains. After an hour or two of struggling against it the travelers stopped in the middle of the road and looked at each other despairingly.

"We shall have to find shelter," said Harlequin. He

squinted down the road, peering with difficulty through the curtain of rain which hid the landscape ahead for all but a few rods. "There is a convent on this road. The signora told me so. Dominican ladies. They have an orphanage. For girls." He trudged on. "Look sharp for a girls' school. On guard, girls! We are approaching. There is no escape."

Another ten minutes brought them within sight of a building which was plainly a religious house. It was perched on a little knoll and the chapel stood at the highest point with the other buildings huddled around it. Drawing his cloak around him and straightening his biretta, Agostino took Gian-Piero by the hand and approached the wicket where he knocked three times.

He was obliged to knock several times more before there was a scrabbling at the wicket. Presently a face appeared, a pointed female face surrounded by a white wimple, and a voice cried, "Who is it?"

"Two pilgrims, dear Sister, drenched and famished. May we beg shelter until the storm passes?"

"Oh, dear me, it's a priest. Oh dear, dear. Come in, Father. How do you come to be abroad in such weather?" The wicket was thrown open and a tiny nun in the black and white robes of the Dominican order bustled Harlequin and Gian-Piero over the threshold.

"A boy!" squeaked the little nun. "Father, you must keep the boy in hand." She behaved as though she thought Gian-Piero might get out of hand at once. "Don't let go of him. This is an orphanage for girls. We never have boys here. Reverend Mother, oh Reverend Mother!"

She had guided them down a passageway into a large and

rather elegant parlor with a fire burning in a grate, a carpet of red wool on the flagged floor and well-polished furniture. Gian-Piero had never seen such a comfortable room, just the sort of room he would have liked in his tower at Rocca. The Holy Virgin, whose shrine stood in one corner of the room, was made of wax with blue eyes, pink cheeks and golden curls. Her robe was trimmed with real lace and the hem was embroidered with seed pearls in a design of lilies which, in Gian-Piero's eyes, was exquisitely beautiful. The place was so clean that it stank of wax and vinegar. These nuns must be made of money, thought Gian-Piero.

"Reverend Mother," squeaked the nun again. "Two pilgrims, one of them is a boy," she piped down the passageway.

As she called, a second door into the parlor opened a crack and Gian-Piero, whose gaze was everywhere, saw a face peeping into the room. It was the face of a child a year or two older than himself, a girl. She wore a white veil pinned around her head but her dark hair showed beneath the veil and a lock or two escaped over the shoulder of her habit. Her face glittered with curiosity. She caught Gian-Piero's eye, her mouth curled into a smile and she laid a finger to her lips. Unfortunately for her the nun turned around and saw her.

"Ginestra! Spying again. Have you no modesty? Back to our novice mistress at once. What have you done with Sister Francesca? If you have locked her in her cell again —" She swept toward Ginestra who shut the door and evidently bolted. Gian-Piero heard the click of her sandals on the tiles.

"Novices, novices," said the nun in a whimper. "Pray sit down, Father. Reverend Mother will come at once. Pray disregard the novices. Boy, you are not to think about the novices. Oh, dear me. And he is such a wet boy." She seemed to think that if he were a dry boy everything would be much easier. However her lamentations were cut short by the entrance of the Reverend Mother, Mother Barbara, who swept into the room and greeted the two pilgrims kindly.

"Certainly you are welcome to stay until the storm is over. Do not distress yourself, Sister Giuseppina. The boy will not interfere with the novices. Come closer to the fire, boy. You will forgive my delay, Father. We were just rehearsing the orphans. We are having a performance this afternoon. I hope you are fond of music."

🐚 FOUR 🐚

MOTHER BARBARA was a Medici on her mother's side, cursed with the sin of pride and over-fond of the arts. Her pride helped her to fulfill her vocation because it required that she do things right. Therefore, her orphanage was well run, her orphans clean and well fed. Her love of music was so strong that all her girls learned to sing. No orphan under her care, however tone-deaf, escaped her clutches without having mastered the skill of reading music. In their off-hours the girls embroidered or cooked or did up the linens or tended the flowers or read *The Lives of the Saints* under the care of the novice mistress, Sister Francesca, who led a dog's life at the hands of her charges. They locked her in her cell and tripped her up with spider webs made of their embroidery silk. They let mice loose in the parlor and filled the wine carafes with ink. They lacked even the most rudimentary virtues but they all sang and some of them played instruments.

"But there, Father, you know what children are," said Mother Barbara, "and girls are in some respects even more devilish than boys."

Agostino shook his head sadly and said he didn't doubt it. "The Mother of us all," he said somberly, "has much to answer for." He took a sip of the dry vermouth which stood on a little table at his elbow and bit into a sweet biscuit. "It makes your work all the more charitable," he continued, "in that it is fraught with so many spiritual trials. Tell me, where do your orphans come from?"

"Alas, Father, the dung heap and the city wall, poor babes, though here and there we find on our hands the children of those who might have done better by them. The unhappy offspring of persons of rank and fortune who have cast off their own flesh and blood, rather than confess to them — and their shame. We pray for their sin and raise their girls in God's service. They come into the sisterhood if they have the vocation for it. Others we place in service and a few marry. But a girl without a portion, however beautiful and virtuous, hasn't much luck in these times. The good Count d'Ascanio-Lisci, our neighbor and a most devout man, has provided us with a small sum for dowries. He is passionately devoted to music. Our girls' choir is one of his charities. We shall be performing for him this afternoon. I trust you will make one of our party."

"Nothing would please me more — and if it continues wet and my nephew and I cannot pursue our journey we shall gladly join you and the count. I am devoted to music. Likewise my nephew."

Gian-Piero looked up in amazement. He would have liked to have been devoted to music but the opportunity had never arisen.

"Ah, the dear little fellow. Such a pretty child, Father."

"Yes, he takes after my adored sister. Her features to the life. And now he is a sacred trust to me."

43

"You are raising him to follow in your footsteps?"

"Oh, assuredly. He shows every sign of a vocation. May I trouble you for another biscuit? And one for the boy? Here, nephew. You may have another marzipan biscuit. Yes, as I was saying, a very saintly child."

"He looks it," said Mother Barbara. "What did you say his name was?"

"Tell Reverend Mother your name, nephew," said Harlequin.

"Gian-Piero," whispered Gian-Piero.

"He is very shy," said Agostino, giving his nephew a poke in the ribs with a long thin finger. "Gian-Piero" — he paused and sucked in his breath — "Visconti."

"A noble name, dear Father," said Mother Barbara, beaming, "and he appears worthy of it."

"Oh he is, he is, the prince of nephews."

"And I suppose you are taking him to Milan," said Mother Barbara. "Florence of course is my home. My mother's family — my mother was a Medici — made Florence the queen of cities and there is nothing in all Italy to be compared with it. Still I am very fond of Milan. Pray give my most affectionate remembrances to the archbishop upon your arrival."

"We should not fail to do so were we actually going to Milan but we are in fact proceeding to Venice. The boy's prospects lie there."

Again Gian-Piero looked up in astonishment. Harlequin flashed a look at him which he could not fathom, and then proceeded with a tale which made even Gian-Piero's most elaborate falsehoods seem the artless inventions of the dullest shepherd boy. He was stunned with admiration. Agos-

44

tino Molino, the elegant city-bred ecclesiastic from a good family, was as different from the countrified parson who had absolved the villagers of Fontesecco last night as wine from vinegar. He was like a wizard in a fairy tale who could turn himself into a lion or a mouse as he pleased. The tale spun on as believable as the rain pattering on the tiled roof.

The deathbed of a certain monsignore was the occasion for their hurried trip to Venice, sighed Harlequin. The monsignore was a close relative and "the guide and counselor of my religious life." Here the voice trembled slightly. It was necessary that they reach Venice in time to receive the good man's blessing. This haste accounted for the bedraggled condition of the pilgrims. Gian-Piero had lost his coat at the inn at which they had stopped the night, stolen by thieves who had attacked them in their beds and had also taken their money. They had been beset by such shocking luck that ten to one the bishop would be dead by the time they had sighted the dome of Saint Mark's. And Mother Barbara knew well that in the great world of cardinals and archbishops deathbeds were of the greatest importance. Mother Barbara nodded in agreement. The dear child's prospects — Harlequin lowered his voice and Mother Barbara's eyes widened — and these prospects were very considerable, depended upon his arrival in time to take part in the melancholy scene. But now his voice took on a more confident tone. The rain was bound to stop and no doubt the Count d'Ascanio-Lisci would be glad to assist the travelers as far as Lucca.

Mother Barbara was quite certain that he would and she disposed freely of the count's horses, carriage and servants. Why, the count might take them to Venice personally. The count traveled frequently in that direction to hear the music of the Red Priest, the great Vivaldi, who was just now ravishing the ears of the whole world.

Harlequin agreed but said that Lucca would be quite far enough. He wouldn't dream of troubling the count for assistance as far as Venice.

"But the monsignore may die," said Mother Barbara, "and the little Visconti's prospects!"

"Ah, it will be as the Lord wills. And the monsignore is very strong. He may linger for some time."

Gian-Piero, listening to this conversation, drinking the chill nut-flavored vermouth and munching biscuits felt transformed into something quite different from himself. He became the little Visconti, a fellow with a future, and lived among the rich and the great and attended those balls and levees with the illegitimate sons of cardinals and the Florentine dukes of which he had read. Somebody might give him that tower after all. How could you be a Visconti without a tower? And he felt a true Visconti.

Harlequin was telling anecdotes of Colonnas and Sermonettas and Strozzis, of Archbishop This or Bishop That. He boasted of splendid friendships, of advice given and received, of expressions of eternal indebtedness and undying affection. He added bits of scandal which spiced his stories as truffles spice a sausage, entrancing the lady-nun in her black and white habit who perched on her figure-eight chair like some sanctified magpie collecting bright shreds of gossip to hoard forever. Harlequin's fancy was inexhaustible. He improvised the entire fashionable world in the convent parlor. The stories grew wilder and taller as he prosed on.

Warmed by the fire and the wine Gian-Piero half dozed, daydreaming that he, the true Visconti, was elected Pope, and that Domenico had turned into a milk white mule with a scarlet and gold bridle. From his post beside the fire he watched the two grown-ups through his eyelashes and while he watched he became aware that someone was watching him. His eyes slid to the paneled door. It had opened a crack. The crack widened ever so slightly.

A face peered around the door. A pair of fierce black eyes fixed themselves on Harlequin. Oh God! She was staring at his feet. Above the black slipper a length of vivid yellow stocking was visible. The little girl's eyes swerved to Gian-Piero and she lifted a finger and beckoned. Silently Gian-Piero shifted his bottom along the hearth and when he was well behind the two grown-ups he rose to his feet and tiptoed to the door. His escape was made easier by the entrance through the door of a black kitten which scampered across the room and leaped into Mother Barbara's lap.

"Ah, little Good-Luck!" she cried, catching the kitten up and fondling it against her cheek.

"An exquisite animal!" cried Harlequin, clasping his hands in ecstasy and darting a sidelong glance at Gian-Piero as the little novice seized the boy by the wrist, jerked him into the passage and shut the door silently after him.

"Now then," said the young lady in a theatrical whisper. "Who are you?"

"Visconti," said Gian-Piero, glibly.

"Nonsense, you're no more Visconti than I am." She waited for this to sink in and then added, "Nor is he a priest."

"Yes, he is. I mean how did you know?"

"Did you ever see a priest with yellow stockings? Come along. Who is he? Tell me his name."

"I don't know it."

"Of course you must know it. You're traveling together, aren't you?"

"Yes. But he never told me his name."

"That's ridiculous. You must be lying."

"I never lie," said Gian-Piero indignantly. "And anyway, what is your name?"

"I'll tell you my name when you tell me yours."

"I told you. Visconti. Gian-Piero Visconti."

"Gian-Piero will do. I'll believe Visconti when I see a reason to. My name is Ginestra. Ginestra d'Ascanio-Lisci — if the truth were known."

"What do you mean by that?"

"Why, I'm his granddaughter, of course."

"Whose granddaughter?"

"The old count's. They've tried to tell me I'm an orphan. But I know better. I'm not like all those others. I'm of the nobility. He just won't recognize me."

"Oooooh."

"And they want to make a nun of me. I'm a novice. Mother Barbara made me a novice because of my voice. But she's *all wrong*. She's not going to bury me and my singing in this tomb. Not little Ginestra."

"You mean you don't intend to be a nun?" asked Gian-Piero.

"No more nun than your priest. That's precisely what I

mean, boy. However that's all settled so there's no point in talking about it. What I want to know is *who is he?*"

"If I should tell you what would you do?"

"Do? What should I do?"

"You might send for the constables."

"You mean —" Her eyes began to sparkle with pleasure. "You mean he's a brigand?"

"No!" exclaimed Gian-Piero. "Of course not. Whatever made you think that?"

"Well, you won't tell me what he is so I suppose it must be something very wicked."

"No. He isn't very wicked. I'm not sure he's even wicked at all — unless —"

"Unless what?"

"Unless it's wicked to pretend you're a priest when you're not."

"I expect he'll get about a thousand years in Purgatory for that," said Ginestra cheerfully. "Unless of course it's blasphemy. Then he could go to hell. But you still haven't told me who he is. If he isn't a brigand he must be something rather *like* a brigand — a pickpocket or a receiver of stolen goods."

"He isn't either of those things," said Gian-Piero crossly. "I should think you could tell by the way he talks. He's a comedian."

"A comedian!" For a moment she had looked disappointed but now her eyes began to glow again. "You mean a harlequin! The devil's cousin?"

"Well," said Gian-Piero. "All I can say is that you're a fine nun. You *want* him to be the devil's cousin."

"I told you I should never be a nun. They keep me here because of my singing. But they'll never make a captive of me. I shall get away. I shall go to Rome or to Venice and sing and sing. I shall sing in the streets if I have to. And my grandfather, the Count d'Ascanio-Lisci, will be so proud of me that he will recognize me and leave me all of his money instead of giving it to his horrid fat nephew. And I shall marry a marchese or perhaps even a granduca and be very famous and everyone will be in love with me and terribly, terribly jealous besides."

She was prancing about the narrow passageway as she talked. Gian-Piero felt as though he were in a cage with a wild animal. He was both fascinated and repelled. Ginestra d'Ascanio-Lisci — if that was who she was — was very pretty but she frightened him. He had never seen anyone like her. His memory strayed back to the Baronessa Ermina Corvo, unattractive but safer than this creature in habit and veil who zigzagged up and down the narrow corridor boasting of a granduca.

There were voices at the door. Ginestra caught Gian-Piero by the wrist and pulled him into a niche. The niche, a wide one, contained a pedestal upon which St. Teresa of Avila stood lifting up her eyes to heaven. Ginestra cast herself on her knees, rolled up her eyes until nothing showed but the whites and froze in prayer. Gian-Piero did the same. Mother Barbara and Harlequin came ambling down the corridor.

"And in the next hour you shall hear our girls sing. The good Father Guglielmo Paradisi, our priest, has composed such a delightful mass for them. And we have a little novice, a charming child, our little Ginestra, found behind the chapel door one winter morning, who is a veritable nightingale. Father Paradisi wrote an Agnus Dei especially for her."

"Liar," hissed the nightingale as the Mother Superior swept past her. "She knows who I am."

"Father," whispered Gian-Piero desperately, "try to keep your feet out of sight."

✣ FIVE ✣

THE POPULATION of the convent assembled with its guests to hear Mass in the chapel just before sunset. It had rained all afternoon but the skies had cleared in time to allow the nuns to walk decorously across the cloister with the orphans, of whom there were twenty or so going two by two behind them like the animals into the ark. The orphans ranged in age from about six years old on up to full-grown women preparing for their final vows. There were also some infant orphans but they were concealed somewhere about the premises under the care of the peasant women attached to the convent.

The orphans all wore smocks of coarse gray material and white veils on their heads. They looked to Gian-Piero's eyes like little saints. Harlequin placed him at the end of the queue and told him to mind his manners.

"They are unaccustomed to rough boys," he said. "Do not tease or frighten them."

He had underestimated the orphans. They were not easily frightened. They pinched each other, made faces, stuck out their tongues, tweaked at the pigtails hidden under their veils and giggled. But as each pair entered the dim fragrant chapel and took their seats in the stalls set aside for them they smoothed the grins from their features, dropped their eyelids and seated themselves primly, ankles crossed, as quiet as a row of buttons on a cassock. Gian-Piero slipped into a vacant stall and caught Ginestra's eye — the left one. It closed and opened again in a measured wink. A titter assailed him. He swallowed it and said a hasty Ave Maria.

Father Paradisi, a very old man, too old apparently to be up to much beyond saying the rosary, hobbled in and took his place at the organ. He raised a paper-thin hand and began to play. He played rapidly and loudly, his head with its big nose bobbing over the keys as though he were a blackbird pecking at the notes.

Craning his neck over the heads in front of him Gian-Piero could just make out a handsome, richly dressed elderly gentleman who was favoring Mother Barbara with his whispered comments. Ginestra's grandfather, thought Gian-Piero. He was a fine figure of a grandfather in a plum-colored velvet coat and a curly gray wig and Gian-Piero did not blame Ginestra for claiming him.

The organ rambled through a prelude, Father Paradisi struck three heavy chords and the orphans burst into the Kyrie. It was a country dance, followed by a Domine Deus which was a gavotte. The Mass was a series of dances, just such as those Gian-Piero had imagined for the sons of cardinals and the Florentine dukes in the now-distant days at Rocca San Filippo. It was everything that he had hoped would lie beyond the confines of the convent of the Poor Clares. How wonderful to be a girl orphan and spend one's days warbling Father Paradisi's masses! The music became gayer and gayer as though it had nothing to do with the words of the Mass. The Credo was a country festival and the Agnus Dei as sung by Ginestra, slightly swinging her hips, was an impassioned serenade. Gian-Piero glanced at Harlequin, who appeared to be listening enraptured with half-closed eyes. But under their lids their gaze was focused sharply on Ginestra. She finished the aria with a sustained trill and glanced around the chapel appraisingly, sensing approval rising in the air around her like incense. The choir took up the Benedictus, a shepherd's medley, and Ginestra pinched the orphan next to her who gave a thin scream but managed to give it on the note. It did nothing to mar the crazy modern mass. Ginestra snapped her fingers in time to the beat of the Amen and gazed yearningly at the ceiling as though she were expecting a vision. "Beautiful!" she whispered.

Others found it less delightful than she did. Gian-Piero, at the end of the queue on his way to the refectory, overheard an old nun murmuring to herself, "Scandalous! Blasphemous! What a way to sing the Mass! And the work of an old man at that. Anyone would think he was past such follies. But some men never grow up."

"Nevertheless, Sister," said a younger nun who was walking with her, "you must admit that Ginestra sang it very prettily."

"Prettily enough," grumbled the older woman. "Prettily enough for a garden fête — or a masked ball. I was merely wondering what it had to do with the Mass. In my day there were rules about those things. The Mass was not a concert. We did not confuse religion with art. The Holy Office saw to that."

The lawless music had made the old nun unusually cross

and she hung over the orphans like a hawk over a hen yard waiting to pounce on the first evildoer. There were so many evildoers among the girls that she finally swooped at random, unable to choose out one among the lot. The selection fell on one quite innocent child whose only offense was to have had her heel trod on by the orphan behind her as the queue entered the refectory. The old nun boxed the girl's ears, knocking her veil awry. The youngster set up a wail and was shushed by her partner. Mother Barbara and her guest of honor, the count, were already at their places at a table raised on a dais, well above the battle. They watched with satisfaction the orphans as they filed in. The cross nun folded her hands in her sleeves and prayed to be delivered from the sin of anger. The girls took their places at a long refectory table and Gian-Piero was placed on a stool at the end of Mother Barbara's table beside Harlequin where he could be conveniently fed from his friend's plate. The novice mistress gave the note for grace, the orphans sang it and the meal was served.

The food was very good. Mother Barbara prided herself on setting a good table. Whatever else their faults, the Medici were not stingy, or so she was fond of saying. The orphans were fed well and the guests sumptuously. Tonight there were both fish and mutton on the table and corncakes in cheese sauce and dried figs and chestnuts. Gian-Piero wondered why anyone would join the Poor Clares when the country was full of Dominican convents.

The conversation at Mother Barbara's table was all of music. The old count chattered on about melodies and harmonies, about canons and descants and when he ran out of breath Harlequin took up the burden. Of all arts, he said, music was the most pleasing to the saints. To hear him talk, thought Gian-Piero, they couldn't do without it. He fluted on, praising this master and condemning that one. He had spent most of his life singing in choirs, it seemed. The old count nodded his curly wig and blinked his nearsighted blue eyes. He was delighted, he said, to have found a traveling companion with whom he had so much in common. He only wished he might prevail on the good Father to remain with him at his palazzo in Lucca for a few days.

Alas, this could not be. The dying monsignore was trotted out and described again. The count would have to content himself with enjoying the company of his new friend on the journey to Lucca. After that they must part. But no doubt they would all meet one day in Venice.

"Indubitably," said Harlequin. "My nephew and I have no plans after Venice."

Later in the little room in the guest house which he shared with Harlequin, Gian-Piero, wrapped in Harlequin's cloak and tucked into a truckle bed, asked, "How do you know so much about music?"

"I know nothing of music."

"But you sounded as though you did."

"It's merely a question of striking the right notes. After all, it was a fine dinner with good wine and first-class company — the best society you'll find in the provinces — so I thought I owed them something."

"But you used all the right words."

"I used the words that the count used. I listen for the cue. Then I speak. That's how I get my living."

The guest quarters consisted of a two-room cottage a few yards away from the convent. The room which Harlequin and Gian-Piero occupied was large and clean and smelled of new plaster and cows. It had housed the cattle until Mother Barbara had built a regular barn. It contained two cots and Gian-Piero's truckle bed. In one corner of the room a votive light burned before a shrine of Saint Dominic. Harlequin, having given up his cloak to Gian-Piero, removed his cassock, turned two somersaults in front of the shrine and crossed himself. He was just about to lie down on one of the cots when there came a small noise at the door, a kind of scratching, followed by a faint mew.

"It's Mother Barbara's kitten, Good-Luck," said Gian-Piero. "He must have been shut out."

"That will never do," said Harlequin. "Kittens do not like the night air." He jumped out of bed, went to the door and opened it.

It was not Good-Luck at the door. Standing on the threshold in her shift, the wind lifting the hair at her temples, was Ginestra.

"Oh," said Harlequin. "I thought you were the cat."

"I thought you would," she replied. "That was why I mewed."

She looked Harlequin up and down carefully and then said, "Aren't you going to ask me in? I might catch my death of cold standing out here."

"In that case," said Harlequin, none too graciously, "perhaps you had best come in. But not for long."

She stepped across the threshold and into the room. "Shut the door," she said and shut it herself.

Gian-Piero in his truckle bed pulled the cloak up to his chin and prepared to enjoy the show. If Harlequin was embarrassed he did not show it. He had returned to his own pallet and was sitting up with his hands clasped around his knees. The light from the votive lamp flung long shadows across the room and made both Harlequin and the girl look larger than life-size. Ginestra went to the shrine; "By your leave, Blessed Saint Dominic." She took the lamp, crossed to Harlequin's bed and held the light close to his face, the better to study his features. He stared back at her composedly.

"Well, Sister," he said at length, "if my face can further your fortunes, it is at your service."

"What should I want with your face? I've got one of my own. And don't call me Sister. I'm only a novice and I don't intend to stay in the convent."

"You were looking it over so closely that I thought perhaps you wanted to buy it. Unfortunately it's not for sale. If it were I'd let you have it cheap and get me a better one."

"I was looking at you to discover if you could be trusted." She gave a short sigh. "But I can't tell. You have a peculiar sort of face."

"It's useful to me," said Harlequin. "I use it to see and hear with and it comes in handy for eating and talking. Pray what do you do with yours?"

She stuck out her tongue at him. "I didn't come here to make jokes. Actually I have a proposition to make."

"Is there money in it?" asked Harlequin.

"Not immediately — but there could be later."

"Money later on never answers. Money comes now or not at all. I am not interested in your proposition."

"But you haven't heard what it is yet."

"It will gain me nothing."

Ginestra, who had been looking at the floor, suddenly raised her eyes and said in a furious whisper, "If you don't listen you may be very sorry."

"Why should I be sorry?"

"Because you're not what you seem and I know it. So take care not to cross me."

"Very well," said Agostino after a moment's pause, "what is your proposition?"

"Tomorrow," said Ginestra, clasping her hands, "you are to reveal to the Count d'Ascanio-Lisci who I am. You are to explain to him that I am his illegitimate granddaughter and you are to tell him to recognize me as his heiress and to get me out of this place and have me to live with him in his palazzo. All this you will do for me and I shall make you rich."

"But what proof have I that you are the granddaughter of the Count d'Ascanio-Lisci? He will never believe me."

"Of course he'll believe you. My swaddling bands were marked with the letters AL. Mother Barbara told me so. She wouldn't tell me what AL stood for but I know she knows."

"Any laundress could have marked them," said Harlequin.

"Nonsense. AL stands for Ascanio-Lisci. I know it does. Will you do what I ask?"

"Suppose I should fail."

"You won't fail if you really try."

"I am not sure that I have the inclination to try. I have no wish to do the count a disservice."

"If you won't try I shall be forced to make you do it."

"Make me!" For the first time in his short acquaintance with him Gian-Piero saw Agostino Molino genuinely nonplussed. For a moment his features were stripped of the many masks he wore and the lean face with its crooked nose, almond eyes and pale firm mouth was naked and astonished.

"If you won't do as I say," pursued Ginestra, "I shall tell them all that you are a fraud, a harlequin masquerading as a priest. They'll put you in the stocks and whip you or perhaps even send you to the galleys, so you will be wise to do as I say. For the boy's sake as well, whoever he is. He'll turn out an orchard thief, I daresay. And will get what he deserves too."

She threw a look at Gian-Piero who quaked under the priest's cloak. It struck him that he could well be accused of stealing. He had stolen Domenico. The penalties for making away with livestock were, as he knew, very severe. A horrible image of himself swinging from a crossbeam flashed before his eyes. It looked very much as though all this folly might lead to the gallows. If the Poor Clares didn't get him for stealing their donkey, Pantaloon would catch him if he tried to steal it back. Repairing the damage would be as bad as leaving it alone. Under the filched mantle of churchly authority Gian-Piero shivered like a jelly.

Ginestra's threats seemed to have left Harlequin with no choice as to what he should do. He shrugged his shoulders and said, "As you wish, young lady. I shall do my best for you."

"Tomorrow?"

61

"Tomorrow, while we are riding to Lucca."

"No. That won't do. I want him to take me away with him."

"It would be difficult enough to break the news to a man that he has a full-grown granddaughter without at least letting him eat breakfast."

"I should think he'd be glad of a full-grown one, rather than some squalling brat. I'm just the age to please him most. Old men like girls of my age. So you will tell him first off or —" She drew the edge of her hand across her throat in a slicing gesture.

"I shall inform him," said Harlequin.

"Good. It's agreed then. Depend upon it. I shall reward you generously."

"In that case I implore you to return to your own cell. I require some rest before I perform tomorrow's impossible task."

"Very well. I wish you good-night. Benedicite." She picked up the votive candle and left the room on silent bare feet, closing the door noiselessly behind her. She left the room lighted only by the moon which shone brilliantly through one little window on Harlequin as he leaped off the bed and threw the cassock over his shoulders.

"We must leave at once."

"At once? But what will they think?"

"It is useless to worry about what they will think. They will think what they please. The point is that that little zany means every word she says. I shall be in the stocks by noon tomorrow if I waste time here. There is nothing for it but to make off immediately. It is unfortunate about the count. I'd hoped to make a new and useful friend. Rich acquaintances are not to be let go lightly but this one must be sacrificed."

He bundled himself into his cloak while he talked, caught Gian-Piero by the hand and together they crept out of the guest cottage and down the path leading to the highroad. The moon was big as a dinner plate, the night was windless and mild. An hour of rapid walking brought them to the village of Sant' Ursula and they stole through it like ghosts. Once beyond the town Agostino halted.

"We have run far enough. We can rest now. There is a hayrick in this field. We shall sleep until cockcrow. Tomorrow we are bound to catch up with the others. And Pantaloon — !"

He vaulted over the fence separating the pasture from the road and led Gian-Piero to the hayrick. Together they burrowed into the fragrant mass and when they had contrived a bed they crept in and both of them fell quickly asleep.

The red rim of the sun lifting above the white crags and the crowing of a cock awakened them. Agostino was the first to crawl out of the haystack. Gian-Piero just behind him saw him straighten up in the sunlight. Then Agostino gave a sharp exclamation as though something had stung him. Gian-Piero gave another. There in the meadow with dew on her mantle stood Ginestra.

☙ SIX ☙

"WELL," said Agostino, "only look at what the Blessed Mother has sent us today! And what do you suppose your esteemed grandfather would say to this, young lady?"

"What grandfather?" sobbed Ginestra. The tears were trickling down her cheeks and as they fell she licked them away like a cat licking its whiskers. At least she wasn't howling, thought Gian-Piero.

"You astound me," said Harlequin. "I understood that you were granddaughter to the illustrious Count d'Ascanio-Lisci and that only the merest misalliance stood between you and a fortune and a title."

Ginestra gave a prolonged sniff and wiped her nose on her sleeve.

"I told you that he doesn't know about that. That's why I wanted you to tell him. He liked you and you could have made him believe it."

"Ah," said Harlequin. "So we need concern ourselves only with Reverend Mother, all the holy ladies and, of course, the ecclesiastical authorities. Snatching nuns from their convents is a serious offense. Gian-Piero and I could encounter some heavy penalties. Truly we are grateful to you. You must turn right around and march straight back where you came from."

"But I can't," screamed Ginestra. "I can't do that."

"Why ever not?"

"Don't you know what they do to apostate nuns? I shall be flogged. I shall have to do penance in a sheet and crawl on my bare knees to the altar every Friday. I shall be walled up alive in the cloister. You've no idea what nuns are. Oh, don't send me back."

"Nonsense. None of these things will happen. You've not taken final vows. The worst you can expect is a good scourging."

"They'll brick me up, I know it," wept Ginestra. "I daren't go back. There's a nun they did it to and her ghost walks the cloister weeping and tearing her veil and blaspheming. If you send me back I shall do the same thing. I'll haunt *you*. You'll wake up in the middle of the night and see me standing beside your bed with my mouth full of straw and you'll die of fright. Oh, please don't send me back. Besides, I've walked all night and I'm hungry and cold. You were in a warm haystack but I was out in the open all night. And now you don't seem in the least glad to see me."

"You are entirely mistaken," said Harlequin. "It was merely that delight robbed me of appropriate speech. And Gian-Piero here is as enraptured as I am. You can tell by the way he scratches. Supreme happiness always makes him itch."

"You're making game of me," exclaimed Ginestra. The tears ceased to flow and she stamped her foot. "How dare you be so insolent?"

"How dare you be so haughty?"

"I shall leave you."

"Do," said Harlequin. "You will save me a world of

trouble. I have a pressing engagement with a troupe of players. They will be going bankrupt without me. Nobody would pay a scudo to see old Schiavullo pretending to be Pantaloon unsupported by me. Gian-Piero here wants to retrieve a donkey which he was silly and greedy enough to attempt to sell. I assure you we have no need of feminine companionship. Go and get yourself walled up alive."

"Why can't I join the players too? There I should be safe. Mother Barbara would never think to look for me with them."

"That's right," put in Gian-Piero, finally rid of the hay inside his clothes. "She'd be quite safe there. They'll think she ran away with a priest."

"I don't want to play farces with nuns —" began Agostino.

"I'm not a nun. I shan't be a nun. I intend to be an actress."

"Contessinas can't be actresses," jeered Harlequin.

"Why shouldn't she be an actress instead of a contessina?" asked Gian-Piero. "If she becomes an actress she won't give any more trouble. And we shall be safe because you won't be the person they are looking for. You'll be Harlequin again. They'll never think of looking for her with the players and so nobody need be walled up alive."

"They will look for her under every stone," said Harlequin speculatively, "unless of course they are so happy to be rid of her tricks and tantrums that they take her leaving the convent as a manifestation of the divine purpose. But you may be right — for the wrong reasons. If we send her back to the convent —"

"If you send me back to the convent," said Ginestra, "I shall tell them that you lured me away with false promises and that I fell terribly in love with you and that you *ruined* me. You could be burned at the stake for that."

"Precisely what I was about to observe," said Agostino coolly. "I am sure you would do just that. What pretty tricks they teach you in these convents! And no doubt I should make a splendid bonfire, the victim of my own unruly passions, and you would enjoy the sight. I know you're fond of excitement. Well, I never could abide the smell of smoke so I suppose we had best be on our way. I have a score to settle with Pantaloon. You are hungry and Gian-Piero yearns to be reunited with a donkey. So on with it, Sister. You must learn to walk. Oh, and kindly remove that veil or you will be recognized."

Ginestra did as she was bid, plucked off the veil and blew her nose on a corner of it and then took Gian-Piero by the hand.

"You can support me if I grow tired," she said.

The journey today was unmarred by weather. The sun shone down on a damp and blooming countryside and a morning's brisk walk brought the travelers within view of a sizable village, defended by a crumbling wall. The bell tower of the church peeped over the wall, its arched windows gazing like astonished eyes at the greening landscape.

A peasant whom Harlequin questioned said that a commedia troupe had passed him earlier that morning.

"They were on their way toward Lucca," said the man. "They had been at Sant'Ursula but there was some sort of trouble there and they did not stop. So they thought they might do a night's business at Castellino just ahead. It's not a league on from here. I expect they're there now. But excuse me, Father, what do you want with those players? They're not company for the likes of you."

"Alas, sir, I have a cousin with them. One Baldassare Schiavullo who plays Pantaloon. His poor old mother is dying and I'm hurrying to fetch him to her bedside. Otherwise she'll cut him out of her will."

"Ah, well. You should find them soon. God grant the old lady a good death. Too bad that decent money is to fall into the hands of an actor."

"There is no accounting for the whims of destiny," sighed Harlequin. "Bless you, my son. And may you also receive a legacy. Come, children. An hour from now you will be enjoying the embraces of your dear Uncle Schiavullo. Fare you well, my good fellow." He raised his hand in a gesture of benediction which reminded Gian-Piero of pictures he had seen of saints ascending into heaven. The peasant doffed his cap and waved them forward on a gust of garlic.

"An enemy might die of the stink," said Harlequin. "Otherwise this is not a well-defended town. I expect my friends will have captured it without difficulty."

"I wonder where they will have put Domenico," said Gian-Piero.

"Who is Domenico?" asked Ginestra.

"The donkey. The one that Pantaloon stole. I hope he will recognize me."

"What difference will it make if he does recognize you?" asked Ginestra.

"It should make it easier to take him back to Mother Matilda. He's her donkey."

"Where is Mother Matilda?"

"In Rocca San Filippo."

"Where is that?"

Gian-Piero hesitated. He hadn't the faintest idea where Rocca San Filippo was. He had lost it two days ago.

"It's by the sea," he said.

"But we're leagues and leagues from the sea," said Ginestra. "Why even at my convent we were so far away from it that I've never seen it."

"But it's still there," said Gian-Piero. "It must be because I came from there. I work for the ladies at the Convent of the Poor Clares."

"Poor Clares," taunted Ginestra. "Aren't you lucky to have got away! Why should you want to go back? Don't you want to see the world beyond the Convent of the Poor Clares?"

If she had asked him this question two days ago Gian-Piero would certainly have replied yes. But judging by what he had seen of the world in the last two days he was no longer so certain. He wondered if perhaps its charms had not been somewhat amplified in the romances he had read. He was beginning to be afraid of the world.

"You couldn't possibly want to spend your life around a convent, a pretty boy like you. You're uneducated and a bit common but that can be put right. Why don't you join the commedia troupe and enjoy yourself — like me?"

"You can sing and act. I'm a scullery boy and that's all I know."

"No, it isn't. You can read. I expect you can write too. You could write stories for me to act."

Now that she had carried her point and was in motion Ginestra's hunger and tears had vanished. Her brow was serene and she walked purposefully as though certain of destination and dinner. Since nothing suited her like getting what she wanted she could not imagine why, if she was contented, everyone else was not equally so.

"Besides," she continued, "the donkey won't mind and the nuns will find themselves another ass. Italy is full of them."

"Mother Matilda was very fond of Domenico."

"Well, she'll like a new donkey just as well. Our Mother Superior was very fond of new things. A new donkey will interest everyone. Nuns have very boring lives."

While she was speaking they had come around a curve where the road dipped straight down between two rows of cypress trees. Olive orchards stretched into the distance on either side of them. At the bottom of the hill stood a shrine to Saint Anthony of Padua and just beyond the shrine stood the gate and the crumbling wall of the old town.

"Now," said Harlequin, "I shall unfrock myself." He stripped off the cloak and the cassock, slung them over his shoulder like a sack and stood revealed in his motley. The sun glittered on his diamond-shaped patches.

"Aha," shrilled Ginestra. "You are the one, aren't you! How anyone could have taken you for a priest! But at least you must admit that I wasn't fooled."

Harlequin replied by laying his finger to his lips and then pointed toward the orchard where several wagons stood resting on their shafts. Snatches of song mingled with conversation issued from their depths, largely feminine and high-pitched. Near the largest of the wagons Pantaloon himself was seated, drinking red wine from a bottle and conning a greasy sheaf of notes, from time to time declaiming remarks in his strong Venetian accent and gesturing like a windmill. A little distance from him a fellow in white silk with a ruffle round his neck was throwing dice with a florid man in the robes of a university doctor. Seated beside one of the wagons was a woman in a most compelling costume, a scarlet satin skirt, a green velvet jacket stuck all over with tinsel stars, and with ropes of colored glass beads around her neck. She was shuffling a pack of cards, occasionally turning one of them face up and jeering at Pantaloon at the top of her voice. As Gian-Piero was to learn later, these people never conducted any business below the level of a scream.

"What do the cards hold for me today, Flavia," thundered the old actor. "I don't know why I ask. They've given me nothing but bad advice for the past month."

"I have the King of Coins here," said Flavia, "and the Hanged Man. You can stay here and go bankrupt if you like — or go on to Venice and do it there. It's all one to Lady Fortune."

"That's because you've put the Magician up your sleeve. Shuffle again, old witch."

"The cards never lie so why should I take the trouble to cheat? The Devil will turn up whether I shuffle or not. You'd best be content with the Hanged Man."

Schiavullo had opened his mouth to reply. The words never came. Agostino Molino, moving in a belly-crawl like a cat toward its quarry, sprang. He leapt onto his colleague's shoulders and rolled him like a bundle of old clothes into a midden at the edge of the little orchard. Flavia dropped her cards and began to scream. The dice players sprang to their feet and from the largest wagon tumbled a woman in a blue dressing gown and dyed red hair dressed with paper flowers. She began to beat Harlequin with her fists.

She was a fat little woman and Harlequin escaped her, Pantaloon and the dung-heap easily. He seized the bough of an olive tree in both hands, swung himself out of reach and then perched in the tree like some huge bird, laughing all the while.

"Schiavullo, you will learn not to leave me to settle with the landlord. Flavia, shake the Fool from your sleeve. There's his card. The rest of the deck doesn't matter. Why, Pantaloon! Listen to you bellow! They'll hear you, you know, and if they hear you they'll find you. The constable at Rocca and the constable at Sant'Ursula can divide you up and put the bits in different pails for the dogs. And if they don't hear you they'll smell you. From here to Venice."

Schiavullo had risen to his feet and did not cease to bellow.

"Sant'Ursula indeed! Much good came of Sant'Ursula. They've got a tribe of murdering brigands there. The pawn-broker was found dead — a dagger through his heart — just after we came there. We were run out of town because of it. Did you expect us to remain and be taken up on suspicion until your Graciousness caught up with us? And in Rocca you were too drunk to move."

"So they didn't like you in Sant'Ursula," taunted Harlequin. "I don't wonder. A commedia troupe without a harlequin! With a Pantaloon who doesn't know a Bergamesque from a tarantella and a Captain from Spain who never learned but three Spanish words and a Countess who has taken vows against beauty — how did you expect to manage, Schiavullo?"

Schiavullo was now standing under the tree, shaking his fist at Harlequin, who added to the old man's fury by sending down a shower of twigs on his upturned face.

"You will be sorry for this," squealed Schiavullo, "throwing a decent citizen into the rubbish pile. You'll pay for this. You'll pay dearly."

"Gian-Piero," shouted Harlequin. "There is your donkey. Before anybody pays for anything, Schiavullo, you had better pay the boy his twelve scudi. He's come all the way from Rocca to dun you. And you've plenty of debts as it is without adding another."

Gian-Piero had been too bewildered to take in much in detail but now he looked to where Harlequin pointed and saw, tethered to a stake behind Pantaloon's caravan, a donkey. He was tied on so short a rope that he could not put his head down to graze. His hide was rough and dirty, there were rope galls on his rump. For a moment Gian-Piero doubted that he was looking at Domenico — this must be some other animal. He ran up to the donkey for a closer look and put his hand under the beast's muzzle. The donkey pawed the ground and tried to nip Gian-Piero's hand, a trick he played when he recognized an acquaintance.

"Domenico," said Gian-Piero, "Domenico. They told me that you would get to be an actor. I'm very sorry, Domenico. I wouldn't have let them take you away if I'd only known —"

The donkey gave a short bray, a curse on his condition. All men were liars he seemed to say. Life at the Convent of the Poor Clares had been harsh and frugal. Domenico had, from a foal, served Lady Poverty but Lady Poverty had seen to it that he was sheltered and clean. He had worked long hours

but he had slept in a dry stall and his food had been rough but wholesome. He had never pulled loads too heavy for him and Mother Matilda had picked an occasional carrot for him with her own hands. The cruciform on his back had been a sign to the nuns that God had once bestrode him into Jerusalem. In the Convent of the Poor Clares Domenico was not without honor. But here amid this cackle and glitter of players it appeared that donkeys did not thrive. Gian-Piero began to pick the cockle burrs off his coat and inspected the sores along his flanks. He must have been pulling that caravan with that huge lump of a Pantaloon drunk inside it.

"Oh, Domenico, we shall run away."

"Nonsense," hissed Ginestra in his ear, "they'll never let you take him away. What do you think you are doing?"

"I'm untieing him. He's never been tied like that. And I shall tell Pantaloon — old Schiavullo — what I think of him and take Domenico home. He can keep his twelve scudi."

"Here you, boy. Keep away from that donkey." It was the voice of the redheaded signora, the one with the blue dressing gown. Her face emerged from behind the canvas like an angry moon and was followed by an even angrier one, that of Schiavullo.

"Let that donkey alone or I shall have you in the stocks. It is my donkey, do you hear? It has nothing to do with you. I have had that donkey for ten years. I want no more trouble from you and your Harlequin friend. I'm not fit to perform tonight. My head is drumming like a hive of bees. I've two broken ribs. They're cutting into my liver this minute. Lay a finger on that donkey and I'll have you before the magistrate and strung up for a horse thief tomorrow morning."

"It's not me that's the horse thief — it's you," exclaimed Gian-Piero furiously. "You stole him from me."

"And where did you steal him from?" asked Schiavullo contemptuously. "Try that on the magistrate and see which of us ends on the gallows."

He whisked behind the canvas with a snort. Gian-Piero looked at Ginestra aghast.

"It's true, you know," she said. "They do hang horse thieves. You'd better let the donkey alone."

"At least I can lengthen his rope so he can graze," said Gian-Piero. He leaned over and whispered in one of the donkey's ears. "I'll find a way. I'll rescue you. We'll run away to my tower and hide there and never come back. But you'd better make an act of contrition to Saint Francis. I expect you've offended him."

SEVEN

THE COMMEDIA troupe was not an organization to be more than momentarily disrupted by a difference of opinion between two of its members. As fights went, the one between Harlequin and Pantaloon had been of no consequence since neither had been killed. Schiavullo had added another layer of dirt and smelled even gamier than before and Agostino was temporarily victorious and therefore popular but his state of affairs was impermanent. It would be someone else's turn tomorrow. Schiavullo's ingenuity would doubtless discover some reparation for the damage done to what he called his honor, and Agostino, to the delight of all, would be disgraced and discountenanced. Fortune was fickle and Flavia with a shriek of laughter flashed the card displaying the turning wheel as Harlequin swaggered past her.

"That for you, Strega," piped Agostino in falsetto and made the horns of the evil eye. Gian-Piero and Ginestra who were dogging his footsteps, did the same, "just," as Ginestra said, "to be on the safe side."

"There's a hunter's moon tonight," said Flavia, "so it's a pity about Pantaloon. You might have played a masque in Castellino. But without Pantaloon —"

"Without Pantaloon," said Harlequin impatiently, "perhaps for once we can persuade the audience to stay through to the end of the piece instead of asking for its money back in the middle."

"You're jealous, Agostino."

"Jealous! I! Jealous of that stinking tomcat. You can thank the saints that I've come back to you. And I've brought with me two twinkling little stars so the rest of you can fatten your bellies for a change. What was the take while I was on holiday if I may make so bold? How many counts, barons, dukes implored you to join their households?"

"We never danced a step," said the fortune-teller, "not so much as a Bergamesque. But it wasn't for lack of you. That was all one to the men-at-arms. We got out of Sant'Ursula before the charlatans had even jumped on a bench."

"They smelled Pantaloon no doubt."

"You're malicious as a snake, Agostino. You've beaten the man. Why do you slander him now that he's down? Schiavullo was drunk and snoring in his wagon. No, it was because of the pawnbroker found dead in his bed. He lived just outside of the village. There was a stiletto straight through his heart. A surprise to all. They had thought it was pure granite and that no steel could pierce it. But it was flesh after all and the till was empty as a clamshell. We had set up the benches but then the murder was discovered and the whole town was looking for the culprit. One of us would have suited very well. Anyway, whoever did it had got clean away through the window not ten minutes before they found the body, by the look of things. So we thought it best to clear off. There was no use staying for trouble. And Schiavullo had already made Teresa jealous over a woman in the village of Fontesecco the night before. So she was glad enough to go."

"Yes, we heard about that," said Agostino. "News travels fast."

"I know about that pawnbroker," said Ginestra. "Mother Barbara had dealings with him. Anyone might have murdered him. He would have had the stars out of the Holy Mother's crown if he could have got to them. God rest his soul." She crossed herself solemnly.

Flavia looked at her askance and then turned a sharp eye on Harlequin. "Where were you? And how did you know about the woman?"

"I have friends," said Agostino. "And Schiavullo is famous. Justly. Old men who chase after young women always are. He's been playing his part too long. There's nothing funnier than an old man in love."

"Won't your cards tell you anything about the murderer?" Ginestra asked.

Flavia looked down at her mockingly. "The cards know but why should they tell? What is it to them?"

"How do they know?" enquired Ginestra.

"How? They know everything."

"*Everything?* Show me."

"You want your fortune told, eh?" cackled Flavia. "Well, show me your money."

"Money? I have no money."

"No money, no fortune."

"No matter," said Ginestra, shrugging her shoulders. "I know it anyway. I am to be a great singer. I've no need of your cards."

"God helps those who help themselves," said Flavia. "The cards know what they know. But what would a nun want with a fortune?"

"Nothing for all I know. Nuns don't have fortunes."

"You should know," said Flavia, "and if I were you I should find yourself some sort of frock more suitable to your condition than that novice's robe. It could get you into all sorts of trouble. Not that it's any business of mine." She picked up her cards and dived under the canvas hood of her wagon.

"You are impudent," shouted Ginestra to Flavia's disappearing backside.

"Same to you, Sister, and many of them," retorted the fortune-teller.

Ginestra clicked her tongue. "Vixen," she said mildly. "Why do you endure such a slut?"

"She's a fine fortune-teller," said Agostino. "I admit that she has the voice of a rusted iron hinge and her features are a series of unfortunate accidents but she knows the cards. When all else fails there is always Flavia. People who throw rotten eggs at Pantaloon like to know what's in store for them. Flavia's filled the till many a time by hinting that there's something to someone's advantage coming up a week from Tuesday."

"I wonder if the cards really know who killed Carmine Chiocciola," said Ginestra pensively. "Fancy, a knife through his heart!"

"Who?" asked Harlequin.

"Carmine Chiocciola. The pawnbroker at Sant'Ursula. I almost wish I was back at the convent to hear about it. He was a terrible leech. I wonder how much money the thieves got. They must have been better than conjurers to have found it."

"He probably got his just deserts," said Harlequin. "And anyway it's no affair of ours. Pawnbrokers perish every day one way or another. Ah, Tartaglia!" He signaled to an individual who just now emerged from one of the wagons carrying the little woolly dancing dog under one arm and over his shoulder a small knobby sack which clinked. "Let us in on the news. What's afoot for the evening?"

"Harlequin! Zany. Embrace me. I would fall upon your neck if I hadn't got my hands full. Wicked boy! What grief have I not suffered on your account. Ungrateful nephew! Have I not fed you with the bread from my own mouth and yet you serve me so! Where have you been while I wept my eyes out for you?"

"Harvesting gold, zany. I planted copper and raised up precious metal. Give me your pennies and I'll grow you a crop of sovereigns."

"I haven't any coppers but I can give you a turnip."

"Turnips, tripe and trollops never yield gold pieces. What else have you got?"

"Cipolino," said Tartaglia to the dog, "I think our friend is lying." The dog barked appreciatively and Tartaglia set him on the ground where he rose to his hind legs and performed a short dance.

"He dances well — for a dog," said Harlequin. "And I've two puppies here who should be up to something. The she-one can howl — in tune. Where are you off to, Tartaglia?"

"To the square — to cure diseases. They're setting the scene for tonight."

"Splendid. We can do *The Misfortunes of Pulcinella*. I've got the children right here. They should do very well. They've no experience of the stage and will be as awkward as goats and Schiavullo and Teresa will have a chance to shine."

"Harlequin, you were very foolish to thrash Schiavullo this afternoon. Neither he nor Teresa are going to forget it. You will pay for your revenge. I admit that they should not have left you in Rocca as they did but after all you were drunk. You would have done better to let bygones be bygones."

"Don't be a fool, Tartaglia. How can Schiavullo injure me? The company couldn't perform without me. If I'm hired by the Duke of Parma tomorrow this company collapses. So stop fortune-telling, Tartaglia. Flavia tells better ones. Are you going to sell that poison in the sack to the local citizenry? We'll help you. It's time these innocents saw something of how we do our work. Come, children. Let us follow the renowned scientist, Tartaglia, into the city."

Tartaglia was a small, pale, redheaded fellow with white eyelashes whose general pallor seemed to suggest that he would have a voice of the same order as his complexion. He looked, as Ginestra said, like a squeaky-voiced man. Not so. As Ginestra remarked later, one should never judge by appearances. He had a bellow like an ox. He sold the contents of his sack, a collection of small green bottles, in a voice to deafen the population of Castellino. Above the bench on which he capered, the bell tower with its two surprised windows loomed like a customer caught unawares and against his will.

"Ladies! Gentlemen! An unprecedented opportunity opens up before you. The chance that you have been waiting for over several lifetimes — perhaps even longer. Here is the great elixir which the genius of the Egyptian alchemists devised long ages ago at the courts of the Pharaohs to cure all manner of illness — everything that can afflict mankind. Here it is, ladies and gentlemen — all in this little bottle — for a handful of coppers. Your safe conduct to health, happiness, romance and riches. Who wouldn't take advantage of this golden opportunity!"

"Will it cure warts?" came a gruff voice from the audience.

"As easy done as said," roared the zany. "Rub it on the wart. Say three Paternosters and the wart will fly to the moon."

"About the romance now," cried a handsome young slattern. "I paid a scudo last year to a mountebank for a bottle of Egyptian elixir and my man left me for a wench with a bleat like a nanny goat and hair like a strawstack. What do you make of that?"

"Ah, my good girl, did you swallow it or wash your face in it?"

"Swallowed it of course. I took the whole bottle. It gave me the cramp."

"There's where you went wrong. You should have washed in it. You can't expect any man to love a dirty face. Take a bottle here for two scudi. Wash your face, say your rosary and your lover will come running or double your money back."

"A good tumble in the river would do as much," murmured Ginestra in Gian-Piero's ear. "I don't expect that there's anything in that bottle that wouldn't kill rats or strip the skin off your face. I wouldn't touch it."

"The others think differently," said Gian-Piero. Tartaglia was disposing briskly of the Elixir of the Pharaohs. The dirty-faced girl had parted with her money and several other women were extracting coins from the tops of their stockings and the folds of their kerchiefs while Tartaglia juggled the bottles three at a time and let them fly as each customer paid. When the bottles were all gone he jumped off the bench and caught up Cipolino, who had been watching the sale with apparent enjoyment, and led the two children off to a tavern which gave onto the square. Agostino Molino was sitting over a bottle of wine. He had a loosely bound book in front of him.

"What are you reading?" asked Ginestra. "I didn't know you were fond of reading."

Harlequin turned his dark melancholy eyes on her. "I read the poets with tolerable enjoyment. Why shouldn't I read if the mood strikes me?"

"I don't know. You don't seem like that sort of person. Do you read?" She turned to Tartaglia.

"I have never found it necessary," replied the zany. "Are you planning to let me have some of that wine, Harlequin?"

"There is not enough for two," said Agostino. "However I shall share it. I have a question for you, Sister Ginestra. It is well known that you are learned but can you ride a horse?"

"I don't know. I've never tried. Is it difficult?"

"Much depends on the horse," said Tartaglia.

"I have in mind a gentle horse," said Harlequin. "Pantaloon has such a horse."

"You mean Teresa's horse," said Tartaglia. "Harlequin, if you are thinking what I think you are thinking you are heading for trouble. Teresa will never tolerate it."

"Teresa is nothing but a bundle of old clothes and a shag of false hair. If she rides into town at the head of the company once more she will send the entire town to say the Stations of the Cross and we shall play to the village half-wit, three babies and Gian-Piero's Domenico. What is a young girl for but to open the commedia? I've had enough of Schiavullo and Teresa. I say that Ginestra shall ride into Castellino tonight and that we shall play *The Misfortunes of Pulcinella*. It will start Gian-Piero off well. He can watch what the rest of us do and get a feeling for the stage. Now here is a scenario. All you need do, Gian-Piero, is to follow the Pulcinella about and make as much noise as possible. Shriek with hunger. Ginestra, I shall tease you for your greediness and you will shriek louder. Tartaglia and Burattino can play along with you as children too. And to open the engagement, you, Ginestra, will be dressed as a page tonight and you will enter Castellino on horseback, waving a sword and leading the whole company to the stage."

"All of this will be charming," said Tartaglia. "It remains only to reconcile Schiavullo and Teresa. Agostino, you must be mad. Neither one will stand for it. I agree that our Pantaloon has a disease that no more than a year in jail would cure and Teresa for ugliness is the devil's mistress. But recollect, Schiavullo brought this company together. He manages it."

"He is managing it into debtor's prison. Leave Schiavullo

to me. He will not attend tonight's performance. Neither will Teresa."

"But how will you stop them?"

"I shall stop them."

"I can tell by your answer that you haven't even planned how to do it."

"Give me until sundown and it shall be as I have said."

He drank off the measure of wine and signaled the land-lord. "I shall take another measure of your best red wine and a bottle of brandy," he said grandly. "A bottle of the best brandy for a friend of mine."

"You may have it if you will give me money for a friend of mine," said the landlord.

"Landlords have no friends. But here is Tartaglia who sprouts money. Give the landlord the money, Tartaglia."

"Not I, Harlequin. Why should I give the landlord my money?"

"Because if you do I shall make you rich and famous and if you do not —" He leaped from his chair and caught his friend smartly by the throat. "If you do not we shall all regret it."

"Enough, Harlequin. This is past a joke!" Tartaglia was struggling in his friend's grasp which was just tight enough to make him uncomfortable but scarcely threatened his safety.

"Just the money to pay for the drink, dear Tartaglia," said the Harlequin, reaching into his friend's pockets and pulling out a handful of coins. "There you are, landlord. Make haste before my friend changes his mind. Now, now, Tartaglia. It's a small price to pay for a change of fortune. After tonight you will be rich and famous. I shall be known as the greatest harlequin since Martinelli. We shall have put Schiavullo in his place forever. Teresa can play scrubwoman for a change and this company will act comedies instead of searching for new ways to lose good money. Thank you, landlord. We'll be off to Pantaloon now and make our peace with him."

He left the tavern with a bottle under each arm and executing a set of dance steps every few yards.

"He's marvelous," whispered Ginestra to Gian-Piero. "He gets everything he wishes for."

"But look how he does it," whispered Gian-Piero nervously. "He threatens to kill you. He did that to me. That's the only reason I'm here at all."

"Oh, but he would never kill anyone," replied Ginestra. "He's really very good. He is going to let me open the commedia tonight. Anyone can see that he has a heart of gold."

"Yes, but what is he going to do with Schiavullo?"

"Oh, I expect he'll make him drunk and shut him up in his wagon. There's your donkey, Gian-Piero. Help me onto his back. If I have to ride a horse I want to learn how boys do it."

She hitched up her skirts and ran across to where Domenico was grazing under an olive tree. Gian-Piero clasped his hands under her foot and she sprang astride of the donkey, her novice's habit swirling around her strong thighs.

"Walk him around, Gian-Piero. Walk him around. Ouch! What a backbone! He's cutting me in two."

"It will be easier on the horse," said Gian-Piero. "There will be a saddle."

Harlequin, watching from Schiavullo's wagon, gave an approving nod. "Hold your head up, Sister. You'll manage very well.

"Holla! Pantaloon. I've come to apologize. Will you drink with me? Here is the very elixir of life. Teresa — loveliest of women. A touch of the grape for you, my beauty!" He stepped inside the wagon and presently Gian-Piero and Ginestra heard sounds of unbridled merriment coupled with protestations of undying friendship. Harlequin had made up his quarrel with Pantaloon.

✸ EIGHT ✸

GIAN-PIERO," cried Ginestra. "Am I not doing wonderfully!" Her nun's habit was hoisted to her knees, her veil flung behind her like a shadow; she was flushed and radiant. "I can ride. Look how I can ride!"

She had kicked Domenico into a jogging walk and had ridden him five times around the orchard when Agostino appeared on the tongue of Schiavullo's wagon with a bundle of clothes in his arms and hallooed to her to come to him. Ginestra slashed at Domenico with her heels and he trotted obediently among the trees. He shook her considerably but could not dislodge her, a feat, as Agostino remarked, which better asses than Domenico had failed to accomplish.

"Now," said Agostino. "I shall take you to the wagon of a friend of mine and you shall dress yourself for tonight. I have Teresa's horse for you. He's in the stable of the farmer who owns this orchard. He is a horse of noble blood. Teresa doesn't deserve him. He has run in the Palio in Siena and was blessed at the high altar in the cathedral there. Do not kick him. Merely sit on his back and wave this sword in the air. The horse knows exactly what to do.

"What ho, Emilia! Emilia, I have a little waiting maid for

89

you. A Pedrolina, a confidante, a spy, a listener at doors, a go-between, a Cupid's messenger."

They approached a small wagon which stood under a fig tree beside a vat of copper pest-killer so blindingly blue that it made Gian-Piero's eyes ache to look at it.

A pleasant face appeared around the canvas flap. The face was followed by a body, or rather by two bodies since Emilia had a baby at the breast.

"Here is your understudy. This girl should do you well at any time that you are indisposed, confined or suckling. And she is a fair young virgin in need of virtuous companionship. I commend her to you."

"Harlequin, isn't she a bit young?" asked the woman laughing.

"Precisely, my angel. Which is why I turn her over to you. For God's sake, Emilia, I've had the brat on my hands since morning. Do the saints take me for a nurserymaid? Children are women's business. And while you're about it let me recommend this boy. He has walked all the way from Rocca San Filippo out of love for his donkey, Domenico. There's faithfulness for you. Now he has found Domenico but he needs a mother. Have you ever had a mother, Gian-Piero? No. I thought not. Neither have I. But those who have them swear by them. So — I have discovered one for you. Emilia, I give you these children. What more can a man do for a woman? Dress la Ginestra for the ride into Castellino tonight. I'm off to church to confess me and to pray that Ginestra doesn't fall off the horse. Give the boy a scenario to read. He can read, by the way. He can make himself useful in a thousand ways."

"He would need to," said Emilia. "What do I want with

a boy, Agostino, or a girl either? I've already got one more baby than I need, bless his little heart!" She gave the baby a resounding kiss on the brow.

"But these are from me," said Harlequin, laying his hand on his heart. "A little pilgrim and the sweetest little nun you ever did see. And heaven only knows who gave you *that* one, although Emilia, I never saw a finer child." He ducked a well-aimed slap from Emilia and backed away from the wagon.

"What will Teresa say?" said Emilia. "Do you expect me to sit still and let her scratch my eyes out for helping you to unhorse her? She'll do that you know, rather than let anyone take her place."

"Teresa is out of harm's way. She'll disturb nobody for the next twelve hours. She's snoring off a bottle of brandy in her wagon. Schiavullo is with her doing the same thing. Into the wagon, Sister Ginestra, and show us how a real commedia actress should look. It will be worth your while, Emilia, I promise you."

"I don't know how you can make it worth my while," said Emilia who had been eyeing Ginestra with a cool, professional glance, "but you're right. She would be a good Franceschina. And we are certainly short of her kind. Go in the wagon, little dear, and put on the clothes. Then I'll explain what you are to do. It isn't difficult. And you, Big-eyes," she turned to Gian-Piero. "What can you really do?"

"Good," said Agostino. "I knew you would look after the boy too."

"He must look after himself. But he's a pretty boy. What lovely eyes! Wasted on a boy, I say. He has them from his mother no doubt. Are you hungry, dear?"

91

"He's famished," said Harlequin, "and so am I." Emilia dived into the wagon and came out with some bread and cheese and garlic sausage which she broke generously with her guests.

Ginestra in the meantime was struggling with the garments in the depths of the wagon. Her muffled voice was impatient. "What am I to do with these? How do I put them on? How do men manage? Which way do they go?"

"You put your legs through them," shouted Agostino. "Leave off the petticoats. You can't stuff them inside."

"Oh, how queer I look! Where do they fasten?"

"Poor girl," said Emilia. "I must help her. Don't let the baby have any sausage. It's hard for a nun to turn into a boy." She dropped the baby into Gian-Piero's arms and disappeared behind the curtain. The baby nestled down comfortably. He was evidently accustomed to being flung about. Harlequin bit off a piece of sausage and tucked it into the baby's mouth.

In a moment Emilia jerked back the canvas and shouted, "Look!"

There stood Ginestra, brilliant in a scarlet and gold surcoat over a pair of sky blue breeches, a broad black hat with an ostrich plume in one hand and a naked sword in the other.

"Meraviglia!" gasped Agostino. "A marquis, upon my soul! And now for the horse."

A fellow called Burattino, in the clothes of a serving man, brought the horse around. It was a small chestnut horse and in spite of having run in the Palio it did not appear very ambitious. Ginestra confidently scrambled on its back and it promptly began to buck. Ginestra seized its mane and clung with her knees.

"I told you not to kick him," shouted Harlequin.

"I shall kick him if I like. He will learn to be kicked," she retorted.

The horse danced around the orchard and then came to a stop so suddenly that Ginestra all but pitched over his head. But her fists were so entangled in his mane that the horse could not rid himself of her. He stood still at last, defeated, with Ginestra defiantly on his back. Ginestra lifted her heels with their charming gold spurs and set him to a canter around the orchard, then brought him to a sudden halt so that he reared gracefully before coming to a standstill in front of Emilia's wagon.

"Horses!" gasped Ginestra. "Give me a horse every time. A horse is the making of a man. I would have all horses be bishops if I could. Did you see how he kicked? But he couldn't shake me."

"The entrance into Castellino tonight should be the finest thing that this troupe has done in a century," said Agostino.

It was so indeed, at least in Gian-Piero's eyes. Cressets blazed and trumpets blared and tambourines jingled. In the grand tradition of the commedia dell'arte Ginestra led the troupe into Castellino. Her horse lifted his knees like a thoroughbred and the applause of the multitude was sweet in her ears. She had found her vocation. From that time forth she included horses in her prayers.

The square was a storm of light and music and in the midst of it all pranced Harlequin. Unrecognizable in his black mask, he grinned a devilish grin which never altered. He was almost never offstage and words poured out of him: jokes which Gian-Piero could not follow but which set the audience

93

roaring. Jokes about priests, jokes about soldiers, jokes about women, about moneylenders and nuns and old men in love and liquor, jokes about family life. When he paused for breath Tartaglia was on the stage, juggling three oranges and turning handstands and Cipolino assisting him with a series of mincing little dances.

The farce, of which all of this activity was a part, was in Gian-Piero's view extremely confusing. In spite of the beauty of the scene — for it seemed to Gian-Piero quite beautiful — he felt himself in a nightmare. He was told that he was to mount the stage for the last scene and he hadn't a notion of what was expected of him. The zanies and the learned Doctor from Bologna were there carrying on impossible conversations, dancing, shouting, tumbling, interrupting themselves with bursts of song, confiding strange and guilty secrets to the audience. Pulcinella was pining for a charming girl — Emilia — but Emilia loved Harlequin. So it was arranged by the learned doctor that Pulcinella would be married to a masked woman whom he thought to be the lovely Laura — that is to say Emilia — but whom everyone else knew to be her maid, Franceschina — Ginestra in fact — who had slipped her breeches for a striped petticoat and doffed her plumed hat for a ruffled cap.

"Now my divine creature, we are to be wedded," exulted Pulcinella, an enormous man in a white smock with a ruff and a grotesque mask with a long, hooked nose. "I am your slave, my lady. Command me to anything. I am hideous, humpbacked and old enough to be your grandfather; but for that reason will I not be the more faithful? Will I not be more loyal and loving? Ah, who wants a handsome, young husband, good only for flirting with other women?"

"How true," chirped Ginestra. "Handsome is as handsome does. It is money that makes marriages. Surely you have enough money to pay for —"

"Pay for horns," interposed Harlequin behind his hand to the audience. "And you can believe me, good people, they come very expensive. Why a good set of horns can cost a man his wife's whole dowry."

"To pay for my pleasures," laughed Ginestra. Pulcinella made a lunge for her. She skipped two steps out of his reach and he stumbled and fell prone. The audience roared its approval.

"I'll make you the happiest woman in Tuscany," bellowed Pulcinella from the floor.

"Happy! And how will you support all the little Pulcinellas?" exclaimed the Harlequin. "They cannot live on air and ortolans. It will give them gas on the stomach. How many mouths to feed? He began counting on his fingers. "One countess, six lovers, six little Pulcinellas! Why that's thirteen and thirteen's unlucky." He did a handstand and came up on his feet in front of Pulcinella who was still sprawling. "Why what have we here? I believe it is an old man. What is the matter, old man? Have you been struck by lightning?"

"No, my son. Merely by Cupid's arrow."

"And what do you love? Let me guess. A jennet! You'll ride her well — a proper man like you. No more than two tons in your stockings. Tartaglia! Burattino! Your master's fallen to the earth and must be removed. He can't rise. No yeast."

Tartaglia and Burattino, wearing striped breeches and velvet jackets, ran onstage and started to heave up Pulcinella.

"M-m-m-aster. W-w-we n-n-need o-o-o-xen," bellowed Tartaglia. As Gian-Piero found out later Tartaglia was distinguished onstage for his stammer, a feature of his performances which the audience found particularly endearing.

"Ah, I see," said Harlequin. "Donkeys won't do. Out then, donkeys, and fetch me a team of oxen." And he caught up a switch and began to beat the servingmen.

Later Gian-Piero was pushed onstage with Ginestra, Tartaglia and Burattino, all of them dressed as Pulcinellas in white smocks and ruffs. A mask thrust over his face half blinded him. He was stifled by the smell of sweat and the strong musky scent of face paint and the smoking flares which lit the performance. In front of him a blackness loomed which roared and surged on the other side of the lights, a many-eyed monster called the spectators. Harlequin carried Gian-Piero in his arms and tossed him to Pulcinella who caught him deftly and embraced him repeatedly while once again Cipolino danced dementedly around on his hind legs. Dialogue exploded all around him but Gian-Piero was mute, envying Ginestra her ability to answer so pertly extempore as though born to this speech. Gian-Piero merely shook his head when a line was thrown to him and felt a flush of fear creep over him but his companions saved him — with somersaults and snatches of song and asides to the audience. He was allowed to run offstage with the others and flung himself into Emilia's wagon trembling and pulling off the costume. Then, wearing his own clothes, he wandered into the orchard and found Domenico tethered and dozing. The donkey's presence soothed him and he dozed beside him until the moon broke through a cloud and awakened him with a sudden piercing shaft of white light. He sat up, aware of someone near him, Agostino lying against a tree and gazing up at the moon. He was wearing his motley and his mask hung leering against his chest. In one hand he held a half-blown white rose. He lay as still as the landscape around him and his dark eyes stared unblinkingly into the moonlight. He looked like a corpse.

"Harlequin," whispered Gian-Piero, half to himself.

"What do you want?" asked the corpse.

Gian-Piero gave a little jump. "I want to go home."

"What home? You have no home."

"I mean to Rocca."

"Why do you want to go to Rocca?"

Gian-Piero paused. He could not say why he wanted to go to Rocca. He had never been particularly happy there. He had spent most of his ten years wishing he were elsewhere. Now he was elsewhere and he wished he were back again in the shadow of his tower by the sea. For the first time it occurred to him that he had actually enjoyed being at Rocca and wishing for faraway romantic places. He had known who and what he was. Here in the faraway places he was not at all certain of these things. Even his glorious lies would lose their savor in this atmosphere. What good was a lie when everything was pretense and fancy? The commedia dell'arte had made an honest man of him. He knew that he was not a commedia actor — he had not the wit, no more than Domenico. And what did these people do with people less clever and agile than they were? What became of those unfortunate ones?

"I'm afraid," said Gian-Piero, "that I can never become an actor like you."

"An actor like me," laughed Harlequin. "But perhaps you could become an actor like Tartaglia — or like Pulcinella."

"No, I couldn't. I want to go home. I don't know what I'm doing here. Neither does Domenico. You should let me take him and go home."

"I'm not stopping you."

"But I don't know how to get there. You should tell me."

"I can't tell you," said Harlequin. "You would lose your way even if I did. You would be devoured by wolves in the hills, set upon by thieves or caught in traps. However, I daresay I shall take you home one day if you insist."

"Oh, will you, oh Harlequin, will you indeed?"

"Certainly."

"When?"

"After we have been to Venice."

"But where is Venice?"

"It is on the way to Rocca."

"I didn't know that. I thought it was leagues away."

"Oh all of that. But it is on the sea. So is Rocca. Don't you remember? Two towns both on the sea — they must be neighbors."

"I suppose they must be," said Gian-Piero scratching his head. "I never thought of that."

"Ah, but you're thinking of it now."

"And will you take Domenico home too?"

"Assuredly."

Gian-Piero sighed. If Venice were on the way to Rocca he must have gone the long way around. He looked at Harlequin. Agostino was staring at the moonlight entranced. Promises meant nothing to him. He gave himself a little shake, broke into a short laugh and tossed the rose to Gian-Piero.

"Are you sorry you came, Gian-Piero?"

"No, but I don't know what I'm doing here."

"Ah, you'll find out no doubt."

"But when?"

"When we get to Venice. There's always something to do in Venice." And he leaned back against the tree and took a pinch of snuff, as arrogant as a marquis who is about to buy the moon and to whom money is no object.

"Tell me a story, Gian-Piero. Tell me one of your lies."

✿ NINE ✿

H E WILL take me home as soon as we have seen Venice," said Gian-Piero. "We will return to Rocca and act all the farces there."

Emilia, who was washing the baby's clothes in a pail, wrung out a length of swaddling bands. "Did he tell you he would?"

"Yes, only a few nights ago."

"Well, Harlequin says many things."

"You mean he tells lies?" said Gian-Piero sanctimoniously.

"You can't really call them lies," said Emilia. "He merely says interesting things, things that people like to hear."

Gian-Piero sighed. He understood the impulse.

"That is what being a Harlequin means," said Emilia. "There is nothing vicious or cruel in Harlequin. He does not intend to deceive you. There is no harm in Harlequin." She winked. "He can't help being cousin to the devil."

"He said we should find Rocca when we found the sea," said Gian-Piero.

"Well, we're still quite a way from the sea," said Emilia.

For weeks now the company had been traveling from hill to valley to hill, stopping in one village after another. Sometimes the village was on a hilltop and the wind shrilled through narrow streets sluiced with rain or dusty in sunshine. Sometimes the village stood beside a stream and the company washed clothes and spread them on the rocks to dry. The villages were much alike although some were more friendly than others. In one little town there was an outbreak of the smallpox and the players fled the infection in a panic. Emilia was terrified for the baby and stopped to pray at every shrine, besides dousing him in holy water whenever she could lay hands on some.

They came to another. It was a queer town, dirty and gone to seed with a black and white striped marble church too large for it. The nobleman who occupied the castle on a neighboring hillcrest was so badly in debt — the landlord in the tavern told them — that he had been forced to marry a deaf-mute twice his age in order to avoid bankruptcy. The village priest had been preaching repentance and the Second Coming. It was generally held that he was mad, and indeed he looked so to Gian-Piero who caught sight of him when they first came into the place. The priest came out of his church as the mountebanks appeared with their benches. He was tall and thin and had a squint. He made the horns of the evil eye and launched into a sermon in the local dialect which Gian-Piero had difficulty in following. The gist of it was that all players were thieves and adulterers, or worse, blasphemers. Fortune-telling was the devil's own art, he thundered, as Flavia swung into view. Indeed the whole troupe had one foot in hell already. They must leave at once or death would be their portion — death and the everlasting fire which gnawed at the vitals of damned souls, giving them no rest throughout all eternity. While he ranted, small flecks of spit flying from his dry lips, two or three persons — Gian-Piero could not tell whether they were men or women — clad only in sheets appeared behind him on the church steps and prostrated themselves wailing so clamorously about their sins that Gian-Piero and Tartaglia took to their heels. The whole village was in an ecstasy of repentance and ready to make mincemeat of any strangers who might divert them from the enjoyment of their misery. The company camped in a copse that night, went hungry and cursed the virtues.

In another town the population was afflicted with the toothache. Everyone wanted his teeth pulled out. The learned doctor was so busy at this horrid task that he scarcely had time for a performance. He invoked Apollonius, patron of dentistry, and tried to get Gian-Piero to assist him with his patients, but the boy had no taste for medicine. The learned doctor complained that Gian-Piero preferred to let suffering humanity suffer rather than lift a finger to help allay its anguish. Gian-Piero turned green at the sight of the pincers which the doctor flourished while expounding on his art and fled to Emilia's wagon where he caught up the baby and swore he had been left in charge of it. He could not be persuaded to leave the wagon until Ginestra finally undertook to help the surgeon, displaying a grim efficiency at toothdrawings which earned her the admiration of all.

Gian-Piero spent a good deal of time with Emilia's baby. It was an imperturbable sort of baby. It hung on its swaddling board from a hook which Emilia would fasten in a tree or other convenient spot and watched the world wag. Emilia was a loving mother but she was a conscientious actress and much of her time had to be spent conning scenarios and inventing and performing her roles. So Gian-Piero minded the baby while Emilia jotted down quotations from the poets, Dante and Ariosto and Torquato Tasso, and interesting bits of business which gave color to her parts. Here again Gian-Piero was helpful. He ran through books to find entertaining or touching things for her to quote. For this Emilia was grateful and called him her secretary. Emilia had first thought that she might find a useful assistant in Ginestra but she soon gave up on that one. Ginestra never assisted anyone save for her brief flyer into dentistry. Her life was the theatre and herself in it.

There was nothing Ginestra could not do on or for the stage. Like Emilia she studied plots and copied them down in a notebook. She too memorized long passages of poetry and declaimed them in order to give more expression to her roles. She made up comic speeches and invented new business. Already she was a champion go-between. She could slip a forged letter to an elderly suitor, disguise herself as two or three people in the course of one play and sing comic songs to amuse the audience while scenery was shifted. Trees went up and walls went down, gardens changed to ladies' chambers while Ginestra warbled. She timed her songs almost to the minute. The scenery was mostly painted boards and moved easily but sometimes somebody lost a parchment or a looking glass essential to the action in a scene and so Ginestra sang to cover the confusion.

Gian-Piero was no good at these things.

"No talent," said Agostino. He had been trying for an hour to teach Gian-Piero to run onto the stage, turn a somersault and then speak a saucy aside to the audience. "Anything will do," said Agostino. "Say, 'Here he comes. You can tell him by his horns. Pantaloon himself!' Something on that order."

Gian-Piero tried it but it did not sound right.

"Try not saying anything," said Agostino. "Wag your head and then do a somersault."

Gian-Piero tried that. Agostino watched him gravely. "There is something wrong," he said.

Gian-Piero cocked his head. He knew that Agostino was right but he couldn't imagine what to do about it. Perhaps if they would write out words for him to say he could learn them by heart and then say them. He suggested this course to Agostino but his friend shook his head.

"Inconceivable," he said. "That would not be the way to perform a play. The scene is set. You must make the words. Imagine how stifled and unnatural it would sound if people insisted on learning speeches that someone had written out for them. Granted that there are such plays, but they are all written by scholars at the university and learned members of the nobility. Nobody listens to them. What I am asking you to do is to tell a story. Haven't you ever told a story?"

"Many times," said Gian-Piero, thinking of Mother Matilda. "But then it was me that was telling the story. I wasn't trying to be somebody else while I was telling it."

Agostino shook his head. "You must learn to be somebody else. The written plays are full of Latin and Greek and good advice which nobody wants to hear. The best plays are spoken — by people like me. That is art. All the rest are lies. And lies, I suppose are what you are good at."

Gian-Piero, when he watched Harlequin in these plays,

knew that this was true. On moon-colored summer nights when the village squares were thick with people and fireflies glittered in the trees and the doors and bell towers of the churches shaped themselves mysteriously against dark skies, the plays came to life. In the crude light of afternoon they were a muddle of sleazy silks sewn with brass spangles, scolding people with garlicky breath and blemished complexions, raw scaffolding and tawdry artificial flowers. But twilight cast a spell. The cressets blazed over women of breathless beauty whose wit and virtue surpassed even that of the ladies whose fates Gian-Piero had followed in the romances he had read in Rocca. Emilia would toss her stoical baby to Gian-Piero and transpose herself into Flametta or Columbina or Laura. The doctor from Bologna would give one last belch and step onstage, all dignity and grandiose gesture. Even Pantaloon, for all that he was usually disgraced and humiliated in the farce, was a figure full of magic and strangeness, a rich townsman with a splendid household from which he separated himself to fall in love with some spirited wench who was "not about to send her chastity to the moon." Ginestra had made up that line and was much praised for it because all lost things go to the moon in the story of Orlando Furioso. The Spanish Captain in glittering armor ranted in Spanish or changed his character and played the part of Spavento or Scaramuccia, half soldier, half madman, hypnotising the audience with his wonderful mimicry of a boasting and vainglorious military man. The mocking zanies, the Pulcinella, and most of all, the harlequin seemed to be supernatural creatures, possessors of as many souls as they had names, the devil's cousins all, impermanent as lightning and nearly as dangerous, dreading nothing and nobody, as though the stage were a wall between them and Judgment Day. They made fun of the Pope and the Grand Duke of Tuscany and the Council of Ten in the Venetian Republic, of English milords and French courtiers and Spanish grandees. The richer and more powerful the man to be mimicked, the more likely Tartaglia would stammer out a libel on him, Burattino would hoodwink merchants and noblemen or Harlequin would make them a laughingstock. Remembering how old Celestina used to warn him that he would be struck by a random bolt for impudence, Gian-Piero marveled how the heat lightning flickering at the edges of the hills and convulsing the sky with spasms of violet light never punished Harlequin and the zanies. The saints in the niches evidently enjoyed the show too much to intervene and so smiled calmly down at accusations of lechery, murder, arson, theft and other crimes too numerous to mention.

The only person who cared was Schiavullo. It was, he said, his company. He did not intend to have it disbanded for heresy, treason and lewd language. Agostino argued that although Schiavullo had assembled the company it belonged in truth to Saint Mary Magdalene since Schiavullo did little or nothing to keep it solvent or even performing. He was drunk and disorderly; he and his ugly old mistress would be the death of any comedy troupe were it not for the loyal support of all the cast. Schiavullo knew better than to match wits with Agostino. Life imitated art; he was always beaten. And if by chance he scored a point against his colorful opponent he was as likely as not to find himself upside down in a frog pond with Harlequin crowing in a tree out of reach.

Since that night back in Castellino when he had drunk himself into a stupor he had found control of his company slipping from his fingers. Harlequin had the real domination of the troupe; it was Agostino Molino who decided what scenarios were to be played and how and where the mountebanks and charlatans were to give their speeches and sell their wares and how the money was to be disposed.

"When we get to Venice," said Schiavullo, "justice will be done."

"Harlequin, Harlequin," said Emilia, "Pantaloon is much displeased. You take too much on yourself."

"Whatever should displease Pantaloon?" said Agostino. "I am not displeased with him. On the contrary, he's quite in my good books lately."

"I thought you were angry with him."

"Dearest Fiametta, how could you suppose such a thing?"

"Well, there was that business in Rocca —"

"But that was the first Sunday after Trinity. And here we are at the ninth. Why should I be displeased with Pantaloon after nine Sundays? I don't expect to be displeased with him again until the Feast of Saint Stephen at the earliest. If possible I shall postpone the quarrel until Quinquagesima. To forgive Schiavullo is one of the duties of a Christian. I intend to perform it."

"That is all very pretty, Agostino. But Baldassare Schiavullo has not forgiven you and he will not do so by Advent, nor yet come Epiphany. He means you ill."

"What have I done to Schiavullo that he should wish ill fortune to poor Harlequin? We've had good pickings lately — all because of me."

"You rolled him in a midden. You've put your little Ginestra on horseback and made Teresa look old and ugly. Teresa does not forgive that. Mark my words, Agostino, Baldassare will be revenged. He'll catch you on a dark night in a back alley."

"Why you are as good a fortune-teller as Flavia."

"Flavia agrees with me. She says the House of God is in your cards."

Gian-Piero, tending the baby, shook his head at these words. They frightened him. He admitted to himself that there was a good deal about the commedia troupe that frightened him. Agostino frightened him most of all. Gian-Piero could never tell what he was going to do or be next, a mocking imp or a smiling benefactor. It was, as Gian-Piero put it to himself, impossible to tell whose side he was on. Was he for himself? He did not seem to care about himself. He would laugh at himself on the gallows, Gian-Piero thought. Perhaps he was on Domenico's side. He was good to Domenico. Once when Schiavullo had beaten Domenico Harlequin had snatched the stick, thrashed Pantaloon with it and then broken it and thrown it on the ground. Then he stood over Schiavullo laughing his head off.

"Do you like Domenico?" Gian-Piero had asked him.

"I like all donkeys."

"Better than people?"

"People are a fallen race. Therefore I like donkeys."

"You sound like a priest. That is the kind of thing that priests say."

"Well, you see I have a vocation. My father was a priest. He left me the vocation in his will. It was all he had."

Gian-Piero scratched his head and Harlequin turned a cartwheel and disappeared into a thicket.

There were times during this queer summer's journey when Gian-Piero thought that he, the baby and Domenico were the only actual flesh and blood creatures in the company. They were what they seemed to be and were incapable of being anything else. All the others changed with the many masks they wore. But the baby could be relied upon to hang in his swaddling board and make demands for food. Domenico would shake his ears and crop what grass he could get. Gian-Piero could talk to the baby and the donkey, tell them that they were approaching Venice and once there they would be on their way to Rocca again. He knew that this was a lie but neither the baby nor the donkey contradicted him. He never told them that he was afraid: afraid of the zanies, of Pantaloon, of Flavia and her coins and deniers, her swords and batons, her House of God and her Hanged Man and of Harlequin whom he loved.

He would look at Ginestra and wonder. She could do everything and she was afraid of nothing. She was like Harlequin only harder, and Gian-Piero was convinced that whatever happened nothing could hurt her. If the crowd booed a scene — and it often did, for Ginestra sometimes expressed opinions in her roles as lady's maid and confidante to Emilia's Contessa or Columbina, that even the audiences, who were for the most part not finicky, disapproved of — she turned and spat at them.

They loved it. They could not daunt her and the crowd adored her for it.

Gian-Piero's timidity amused her. "Afraid of fat housewives and farmers!" she jeered, "and a pack of cards. What kind of a boy are you?"

Gian-Piero hung his head and his beautiful gray eyes filled with tears.

"I'm not afraid of those," he lied.

"Then what are you afraid of?"

"Of Venice," he said finally. "What is to happen to us in Venice?"

"Nothing at all," said Ginestra flatly. "What should happen to us in Venice?"

"But what is Venice? What is it like? If it is so near to Rocca why didn't we ever find it before and why has it taken us so long to get there?"

"Venice," said Ginestra portentously, "is where the money is. It is under water."

"My God," said Gian-Piero. "How shall we breathe?"

☒ TEN ☒

IT SMELLED like a sewer and looked like Paradise. Airy domes and frail towers, enskied against the clouds, shimmered again in the sleek waters of the canals. They came to Venice by barge through the salt marshes, passing among the islands, the stench rising around them like something solid. The bargemen bargained like Charon over a cargo of lost souls and for some time it looked as though the only creature who would set foot in Venice would be Domenico whose usefulness there was doubtful. The bargemen would take them to Venice, they said, for the price of a donkey. For once Gian-Piero found himself on the same side of the fence as Schiavullo. The old actor painted such a heartrending picture of the attachment between the boy and the donkey that Gian-Piero quite loved him and even the bargemen, who were drinking heavily during the bargaining process, were moved to accept a lesser but still exorbitant fee, largely paid by Emilia. She remarked later that she always had something put by for such emergencies. "I can't bear to see children cry," said Emilia. "Better to pay a little and avoid unpleasantness."

"Emilia, you have a heart of pure gold," said Baldassare Schiavullo. "I shall owe it to you."

"That you will, you old scoundrel," replied Emilia. "I'll

add it to the account. In any case I did it for the child, not you."

The company took rooms above a lace shop in a tiny street behind the church of San Giorgio degli Schiavoni and arranged to stand watch in shifts over their gear piled in the square.

In the evening Gian-Piero and Ginestra stole into the great square of Saint Mark to gaze at the cathedral and to marvel at the bronze chargers of Constantinople shining under the moon and gauzed over by the mist rising from the waters.

"Oh, the horses!" gasped Ginestra. "Give me your blessing, horses. You are the most beautiful things in all Venice."

The square was as busy on a fine moonlit night as a Monday morning market. Nobody ever went to bed here it seemed and the more he looked the more Gian-Piero believed it. How could anyone sleep while such scenes were unfolding? Gondolas slid through the waters, smooth as seals, and the boatmen delivered elegant crowds of merrymakers to brightly welcoming doorways; ladies, masked and veiled, lifted their brocades to display clocked stockings and scarlet slippers as they stepped from the lilting boats into worlds of music and flowers.

"Soon we shall be invited to one of those palaces," said Ginestra, "and I shall have a black velvet hat and one of those veils and gold clocks on my stockings. I have just the legs for gold clocks."

With a bellow of bronze, heroic figures strode forth from the pinnacle of the campanile and struck the hour, incidentally striking even Ginestra into silence. She crossed herself solemnly and counted the strokes of midnight. She and Gian-

Piero stole into Saint Mark's and said an Ave Maria to ward off danger. Neither one could quite believe that those metal giants might not decide to come down from the tower and chase them out of the square.

But once the hour was struck the metal giants rested content and Ginestra and Gian-Piero, hand in hand, flitted like mice through streets velvet black or suddenly alight with torches as parties of people clustered together or broke apart. Just before dawn they found their way back to San Giorgio and, hesitating to arouse the rest of the company, they crept under one of the wagons and slept on a pile of costumes until late in the morning. At noon Agostino called Gian-Piero to help with the setting up of the scaffolding for the performance.

"Come, mountebank, there is no time to waste," he said. "Our days of idleness are over. There are other companies here and every man jack of them is ready to cut our throats. If we are ever to get ourselves attached to a nobleman's household or invited to play in France we must do better than the others. We must cut their throats first." He was interrupted by a howl from Schiavullo calling for Gian-Piero to come and feed the donkey who was gnawing at the wagon out of sheer hunger. Gian-Piero scrambled off to attend to this task. Although Schiavullo claimed the donkey as his own he was glad to leave its care and feeding to Gian-Piero and over the weeks he had proved less possessive of this valuable beast than he had at first appeared to be. The donkey was useful to him when he wished to make a brief jaunt to the nearest tavern. Domenico also gave him prestige. When drinking with new acquaintances Schiavullo usually referred to him as "my horse," and when really drunk he called him "my Arab." Apart from these occasions Gian-Piero had control of the animal and might do as he liked with him. Here in Venice there was little for Domenico to do and Gian-Piero was puzzled as to how to feed him in a city composed entirely of stone and water. On one occasion he begged money of Tartaglia and bought Domenico some discarded vegetables from a barge on the Grand Canal. Later he found that he could usually persuade a bargeman to take him in return for an hour or two of labor to the salt marshes where Domenico could enjoy the long sea grasses in one of the stinking bogs at the edge of the town.

"There is more pleasure to be had in one square in Venice," said Agostino, "than in all the palaces of Europe."

Gian-Piero saw with his own eyes that this was a fact. In every square, as Agostino had said, other commedia troupes played their farces. Flutes and hautboys echoed from narrow street to sunlit, flower-decked square. There were more goods to buy than there could possibly be people to buy them. The riches of Venice surpassed even the imaginations of the writers of books. There were silver shops and lace shops, shops full of glass blown into dolphins and swans and lions and lilies. In the squares vendors sold oranges, peaches, figs, sausages and chestnuts. Gian-Piero and Ginestra managed to scavenge quite a number of these delicacies and they moved about Venice, eating. In the Rialto they watched narrow-eyed bankers and Jewish moneylenders haggle with gentlemen on the verge of bankruptcy or with masked ladies whose dealings at the card tables had brought them into the power of the Hebrews. They moved to the gardens of the Giudecca and to the very edge of Venice where the tide drew away from the Dogana flaunting its golden ball.

With the juice of overripe oranges running down their chins they tiptoed into the great white church of Santa Maria della Salute. They watched argosies set out from the quays to trade all over the Mediterranean, and they stood beneath the gonfalon of Venice with its crimson lion to watch all the splendid people of Gian-Piero's dreams — and more than he could ever have dreamed of — pass on their way to a mysterious happiness in the villas of the Euganean hills. There were English milords with mastiffs on the leash and French fops who masked the stink of summer sweat with perfumes you could smell streets away. There were blackamoors in turbans, superb cardinals and modest abbesses. There were travelers from the German palatinates who had come to look

at the paintings in the palaces and who were prepared, even though they were heretics, to sit for hours in the churches listening to the music. Venice rang with music. They said that the devil himself inspired the Venetian composers.

"Religion is not a serious thing here," said Harlequin. "Even the Jews are tolerated. Art and politics are more important."

There were traders from the Turkish provinces and sailors from Scotland and Sweden and even from Muscovy — these had formidable beards and looked sullen and confused. Once Gian-Piero saw some yellow men from Cathay. They had slant eyes and pigtails and their faces were unfathomable. There were also beggars, cripples, blind men, dogs, cats, rats, and an all-encompassing smell of rotting fish.

Gian-Piero joined other urchins in jumping from the quay

under the Ca d'Oro and swimming about in the dirty water. It was cooling on a hot day. He began to stink of fish himself and Agostino took to holding his nose when he came in sight.

When Gian-Piero reminded him that now that they were in Venice they must be close to Rocca, Harlequin agreed. "That is true. There is only one difficulty."

"What is that?"

"Have you observed where the sun sets?"

"It sets behind the hills," said Gian-Piero.

"Precisely. And in Rocca it sets in the sea. We've come to the wrong sea."

"But how are we to get to Rocca?"

"Quite simply. We must merely make the sun set in the sea."

"But how can we do that?"

"We shall make application to the clock tower."

"The clock tower?"

"If a man could make the creatures come out of the clock tower then the clock tower, which lives by the sun, can persuade the sun to set where it wills it. Address a letter to the lords of the clock tower."

"He's making game of you," said Ginestra. "He never intended to take you back to Rocca. He merely said he would so you wouldn't make trouble for him. Agostino is like that. He hates trouble, but he doesn't mean to be cruel. Perhaps, some day when he gets rich he will take you home."

"But whenever will Agostino be rich?"

"Oh, it could happen any time," said Ginestra. "Why don't you amuse yourself as I do and forget about things. It's the only way to live. All this remembering is bad for the liver.

Come with me to the Campo Santo. They are playing *The Jealous Old Man* there and I want to watch it."

Several of the commedia troupes which were occupying the city were great and famous companies with such properties and costumes as to make Gian-Piero's acquaintances look extremely shabby. These people played with such grace, style and wit, gave vent to such polished phrases, danced with such courtly grace and dueled so expertly that Gian-Piero could scarcely credit his eyes and ears. Surely these people were not *actors!* Ginestra from time to time contemplated bolting from her present protectors to the company which performed under the protection of the oligarchs of Venice but Emilia persuaded her against the idea. She was not ready for these grand people, who ten to one would be taking themselves off to Paris come winter anyway.

"But I should like to go to Paris," said Ginestra.

"No, you wouldn't," said Emilia. "They speak nothing but French there and the French are a harsh people. If they shouldn't like you they would howl you off the boards and you would starve in the streets. You're better off here."

"Working for Schiavullo and Teresa? I shall never be allowed to play proper parts as long as that old fright is allowed to strut about in grease paint, screeching her head off."

Although Gian-Piero was not inclined to notice, matters were amiss with his company. There were too many diversions in Venice for a small provincial troupe to attract much attention. The money was not pouring in and Schiavullo began to declare that if affairs did not mend the company would shortly become familiar with the pangs of starvation. They would be reduced to eating Domenico or one another.

"If you would simply retire, Pantaloon," said Agostino, "we might yet survive, but as long as you and Teresa persist in adding to the sum of human misery with your truly execrable presences what can the rest of us expect but a wolf in the belly?"

It seemed to Gian-Piero that Harlequin never lost the opportunity to bait Pantaloon — without, as far as anyone could see, bearing any particular malice toward the old actor. He teased him onstage and bullied him off. He interrupted Pantaloon's scenes with horseplay and distracted the audience from Teresa's singing, mocking her gestures in asides to the audience and walking around her on his hands when she was reaching for her high notes.

"Harlequin, you are very foolish," said Flavia for the hundredth time, cutting her cards as she spoke. "And in Venice too. It is not as though you were in a country village. Here in Venice people disappear. Schiavullo has only to hint that you hate the syndics or have picked a pocket to find an honest fellow to get rid of you for him. What do you think the canals are for? Or the Bridge of Sighs? They hanged three strangers day before yesterday in the Campo dei Pozzi. Nobody knows why. But somebody didn't like them. They're rotting there now."

There was no doubt in Gian-Piero's mind that Pantaloon and Teresa hated Harlequin with an uncommon hatred. It showed in their faces. They watched him with narrowed eyes and whispered together when he passed as though planning something. They were not fond of Ginestra, or for that matter of Emilia or Tartaglia either. They were indifferent to Gian-Piero. He did not act and so was scarcely human, entitled to

120

no more consideration than Domenico, whom they abused. They knew that Agostino was fond of the donkey and they beat the beast because they were afraid to touch the man. Because Gian-Piero was of little account, they spoke in front of him as though they did not believe that he understood them. He was well acquainted with the nature of their feelings.

"Angostino is an incubus," said Schiavullo to Teresa. "I swear he is truly the devil's cousin." Gian-Piero, half-asleep on a pile of straw in a corner of the lace merchant's room, came full awake.

"All harlequins are of the devil," said Teresa. "Get rid of him."

"And have him join Montefiore's troupe in the Piazza San Marco? He will take all our secrets with him. He will steal all our scenarios."

"I didn't say dismiss him," said Teresa. "I said get rid of him."

"But how shall I manage that? I can't simply drop him in the canal."

"Nobody suggested that you should do anything so foolhardy. Don't lay a finger on him. Just let the palace guard do it."

"My dear Teresa. How can I persuade them to attack Harlequin? He is nothing to them. And I haven't the money to pay for it. These things come high."

"Where was Harlequin the night the pawnbroker was murdered in Sant'Ursula?" asked Teresa.

"Why, I have no idea. It was a day or two later that he caught up with us, wasn't it?"

"Fool! Zany! What difference does it make? I tell you the

man's a murderer. They don't want his kind here. Why, he could have come here to plot against the republic. The pawnbroker was in Sant'Ursula. Harlequin was in Sant'Ursula. He cut the man's throat as sure as you are a greedy cuckold."

"Cuckold, my dear?"

Teresa gave a harsh laugh. "What is so contemptible as an old man in love?" and strutted off to address herself to her looking glass. Her derisive laughter floated through the little room. Gian-Piero sat up and began to pull straw out of his hair. Schiavullo took no notice of him. His face was puckered with anger and he gobbled for words.

"If you think I'll take that from you . . ." he said slowly, apparently unable to think of a line.

Again her laugh. They seemed to be playing their commedia roles for Gian-Piero's benefit. They had lost themselves in their characters to such an extent that they had forgotten how to quarrel except in the speeches assigned to the masks they wore.

"So Harlequin is your paramour," said Pantaloon fussily. "I shall kill him."

Teresa laughed again. "You couldn't kill anyone."

"Then I shall find someone who can."

"That will be sending for sorrow."

They disappeared down the rickety stairs leading to the street leaving Gian-Piero to ponder this conversation. He forgot it soon enough. As Ginestra had advised him to do he was living in the present and in the city. He drifted downstairs and into the Church of San Giorgio to follow once again the fortunes of Saint Ursula and her eleven thousand virgins around the walls of the church. His mind flitted back

122

to the village of that name and he tried for a moment to recall just where he had been at the time of the murder. When the church grew too dark for him to see the pictures he took Domenico on a twilight tour of the town, over hidden bridges and into a dusky square where he paused outside a stately building to listen for the music. He had come here before and there was always music to be heard. It seemed to seep up from the stones.

Though he did not know its name anyone could have told him that the place was the Hospice of the Innocents. Tonight his curiosity had the better of him and he paused below one of the windows to listen and to discover if he could what manner of company was kept here. Then an idea occured to him. He maneuvered Domenico under a window and found that by standing on the donkey's back he could just barely see inside.

Through the grille he saw a full orchestra of young girls plucking, blowing and twanging away at instruments which seemed nearly as large as themselves. They were led by a man, a vivid and unmistakable man who seemed large enough to encompass them all. By comparison with their littleness and pallor he looked like a column of fire. His hair was flaming red like a burning cock's comb. The girls played at top speed and very loudly to a small audience among whom Gian-Piero discerned a face which struck him as vaguely familiar. Peering through the candlelight Gian-Piero seemed to be recalling a dream. It was a dream of a conversation overheard. The Red Priest — the Red Priest of Venice, so great a composer that the devil himself listened to him — the great Vivaldi. Gian-Piero wondered what the devil made of all those girls.

Who had spoken of the Red Priest of Venice? Ginestra's grandfather. That was the person he was gazing at: the Count d'Ascanio-Lisci. In a black velvet cloak, he was listening enraptured to a group of young girls who puffed out their cheeks on bassoons and plucked at the huge strings of contrabasses.

Gian-Piero slipped astride Domenico. He crossed himself with relief. Nobody had observed him peering in at the window. However would he have explained to the count his appearance at the grille? He was supposed to have been acolyte to a priest when they had last met. His ears still ringing with the Red Priest's music, Gian-Piero urged the donkey back toward the Campo Santo. It was still fairly early in the evening and the lights were beginning to shine above and below the canal waters. The cry of the watch, *"Per l'area buona guardia,"* rippled across the lagoon. He turned into a darker street. It was a lonely one and he was conscious of no sound save the music in his ears and the distant trilling of the doves in the next square. He wanted to find Agostino and tell him about the music. And while he was about it he might as well tell him about the conversation he had heard between Pantaloon and Teresa.

The street which had been so quiet suddenly crashed into fury. A brawl had broken out in a tavern at the end of the alley. Gian-Piero heard blows fall and cries for the watch. Then a figure broke from the angry knot of people collected at the door of the tavern and fled toward Gian-Piero.

"Murder!" shrieked a voice. Someone was thundering toward him, a huge old presence, reeking of wine and onions. He felt the sweaty satins and the weight of Pantaloon's frame knocking against the outer wall of the tavern. The actor was drunk and squealing with anger or fright or both.

"Murder, stop thief! Call the guards!" he roared.

The watch met the old man at the end of the street. Two men-at-arms ran toward the tavern. Schiavullo was waving his arms and seemed to weep.

"Take him. He's a murderer. And he plots against your state. He has already robbed one man of his life. Ask them in Sant'Ursula. Who murdered the pawnbroker? Take him or none of us are safe in our beds."

Gian-Piero caught the donkey and ducked into an alley. The crowd was far too busy apprehending Schiavullo's would-be slayer to notice Gian-Piero. The tumult ceased and Gian-Piero decided it was time to venture back to the company.

He came in view of San Giorgio as the moon was starting up behind the bell tower. He slipped into the lace shop and up the rickety stairs in search of Emilia. He was hungry and she always had food for him. He found Ginestra, her hair in papers, her face half-painted and her stays unlaced.

"Isn't it time you were dressed?" he gasped. "Aren't you acting tonight?"

"Dressed for what? Well, I suppose you don't know what's happened. You never do. Why don't you ever know what's going on?"

"What *is* going on? Why isn't there any play?"

"Harlequin has been taken up by the watch. He tried to kill Schiavullo in a tavern and they've taken him off to prison."

"But he didn't kill Schiavullo. I saw him myself." He

125

stopped — Sant'Ursula sprang to mind. The conversation he had overheard was not part of a farce after all.

"Pantaloon has informed against him," continued Ginestra. "He told the bailiffs how the pawnbroker was murdered. And he says that Harlequin came all the way to Venice to kill the Doge. They'll hang him without a doubt."

"Hang him! For the murder of the pawnbroker! But I was with him and he never went near the pawnbroker."

"Tell them that and they'll hang you too," said Ginestra. "If I were you I'd run away."

"But I can't do that. They mustn't hang Agostino."

"Oh, but they must and they will."

"No they won't. I shall go to your grandfather and tell him all about it. He'll remember Harlequin. He'll know he couldn't have done the murder."

"My grandfather!" exclaimed Ginestra. "What are you talking about? I have no grandfather."

ELEVEN

THE LITTLE upstairs room over the lace shop was dimly lit by two tallow candles. A handful of players — what remained of Schiavullo's company — sat at a dilapidated table eating a meager meal of bread and cheese of which there was not enough for Gian-Piero. Flavia, Tartaglia and Emilia were railing partly at Teresa and Schiavullo, partly at each other. Five nights had passed since Agostino had been taken. There had been no performances since that fatal evening. Pulcinella had left the company along with the Doctor from Bologna, the Captain from Spain, Burattino, Pedrolino and all the zanies.

"But what would you do?" whined Schiavullo. "The fellow tried to choke me to death."

"Harlequin never tried to choke anyone to death," snapped Tartaglia. "This is your revenge because you were tossed in the midden. This is your spleen because you are too old and too ugly to appear as anything but a mute at a funeral. Now we must all starve to appease your spite and the envy of that harridan of yours. Alas, poor Harlequin! That ever he must come to this! A fine, thriving young fellow to hang up like old clothes!"

"They won't hang him," piped Gian-Piero stubbornly. "I

was with him the night and the day the pawnbroker was killed. I know he never committed a murder."

"You will keep your impudent mouth shut," shouted Schiavullo and fetched him a clout over the ear. "You know nothing at all. Molino has confessed to everything — both to the murder in Sant'Ursula and to plots against the Venetian state. And since he has admitted to two crimes he must be guilty of at least one of them and either one is enough to hang him. So there is no use in your running about spreading lies. Everyone knows that you're a storyteller."

"But why did he confess?" exclaimed Gian-Piero.

"They put him to the rack," said Tartaglia. "One turn did it. Agostino was not designed by the Creator for suffering. He confessed to everything that was asked and invented several other crimes which they had never thought of. Schiavullo, you will be impaled on the devil's fork through all eternity for this."

"I tell you he went for my throat. He drew a dagger and held it before my eyes. I thought I was at my last gasp."

"The rack," whispered Gian-Piero. "The *rack!*"

"And so they will hang him," pursued Tartaglia. "It is a great loss. He had talent."

"They mustn't hang him," said Gian-Piero. "He *shall not be hanged.*"

But Flavia said they would hang him. It was in the cards. She had always prophesied it. She had warned Agostino time and again.

Teresa said they would hang him and good riddance.

Emilia said they would hang him and life was like that. The good die young.

128

Teresa wanted to know what was good about a gallows bird.

"They won't hang him," screamed Gian-Piero. "I shall save him. I shall go to the Count d'Ascanio-Lisci. I shall go to the great Vivaldi. They'll hang you, Pantaloon, for stealing my donkey and swearing false oaths. But they won't hang my Harlequin." Schiavullo had risen to collar him and Gian-Piero bolted from the room and down the stairs hearing Pantaloon's shouts and Teresa's laughter behind him.

"Let him go," he heard her say. "He's mad as moonshine. He believes all his own stories. Nobody else will, you can depend upon it."

In the square the little scaffold stood partly dismantled and there was nobody about save one blind beggar wailing for alms and Ginestra sitting among the planks and crying.

"You must tell them what you know," said Gian-Piero. "You must tell them that all the time someone was murdering the pawnbroker Agostino was having dinner at your convent with Mother Barbara and your grandfather."

"He's not my grandfather," sobbed Ginestra. "Nobody at our convent ever had a grandfather. I just made all that up to please myself. I wanted to be different from the other girls."

"But he saw Agostino," said Gian-Piero. "Anyway it doesn't matter what you made up. The Count d'Ascanio-Lisci is right here in Venice listening to the music of the Red Priest and I can take you to him. Even if you aren't his granddaughter he will remember you because he liked your singing."

"I can't. I shall be punished. I'm afraid to go."

"But you're usually so brave."

"Of course I'm brave if it's only a play. But this is real. I don't know anything about the count. He might be angry and send me to prison or back to the convent."

Gian-Piero rose from where he crouched on the cobblestones beside Ginestra. "I am going to see him," he said.

"See who?"

"Agostino. Harlequin."

"But how will you find him?"

"I don't know. But if he could find Venice I expect I shall find him."

"Give him my love," said Ginestra. "I am most truly sorry that he is to be hanged."

"I shall tell him so," said Gian-Piero.

It took him two days to find the prison where Harlequin was lodged. He first tried the famous one near the Doge's palace but learned at the Bridge of Sighs that this prison was only for important people. So humble a felon as Gian-Piero's Harlequin languished in something far less infamous. Leading Domenico by the halter he searched Venice, enquiring of everyone whose attention he could gain for *the* prison, *any* prison, *all* prisons. He mistook one set of directions, and took a trip on a barge to Murano and saw the caves of molten glass and the glassmakers at their magical task. But there was no prison. The mistake cost him all the money he had and thereafter he fed himself on refuse picked up on the quays. The interesting lords and ladies looked less and less interesting as the hours of searching passed. They began to seem like flat painted characters against a flat painted scene, people whose lines were written for them. The gorgeous palaces and delicate bridges blurred into piles of brutal stone and pools of slimy water through which he picked his way without hope. But finally he found himself under the wall of a small but forbidding fortress and learned that the place held some of the cleverest thieves in Italy as well as murderers, coiners, forgers and divers enemies of the state. The guard whom he questioned was pleased to tell him that one Agostino Molino, a harlequin from a commedia troupe, was certainly there and was to be hanged in the square outside the prison on Monday morning.

"A harlequin at a rope's end you seldom see, more's the pity," said the guard. "It should be a fine sight."

In the grisly shade of the prison tower Gian-Piero paused to consider what he should do. It was customary, he knew, to bribe jailers but he had no money.

"Domenico, what shall I do?" Domenico pawed the cobblestones. Another guard, not his first informant, lolled against the wall and told Gian-Piero to state his business or be off.

"My business is with Agostino Molino," said Gian-Piero, quaking.

"Well, what are you paying?"

"I've a good donkey here," said Gian-Piero. "He's strong and he's willing."

The guard shrugged his shoulders. "He may be so but who needs him?"

"He would serve you well. He's very loyal."

"What do you want with Molino?"

"I must see him. He's condemned for a murder he didn't do."

"Too bad. But that was up to the judges. They know what they're doing. And he confessed."

"But he was tortured."

"Some don't confess. However it's all one. They hang the stubborn ones too. But I'm a merciful man. If he's to die on Monday I suppose it's only decent to let his family in to say good-bye. I daresay you're some relation?"

"Yes," said Gian-Piero. "I'm his brother. And he's been like a father to me."

"There now," said the guard. "It's enough to make a man weep. All right. I'll take the donkey and you can go in. I'll give you half an hour."

And so for the second time that year Gian-Piero sold Domenico, and was admitted to the courtyard of the prison. A turnkey led him through the desolate yard, through a heavy door studded with brass nails and into a gallery so dim that he almost tumbled down the flight of stone stairs leading to a kind of pit where the condemned were housed. They were for the most part huddled against the walls, chained by the ankle and in some cases by the wrists also. The place smelled violently. It was a miracle that anyone could remain alive here for two days together.

"Gian-Piero!" He turned at the sound of the familiar voice. His friend, chained to a ring in the wall, lay on a heap of filthy straw. He was almost unrecognizable. The skin was stretched over his skull like parchment. His serpent's eyes were lightless in their sockets. He seemed three parts dead. It struck Gian-Piero that under all the masks the real face was that of a hanged man.

"Gian-Piero, why have you come?"

132

"I came to tell you that I am going to save you," replied Gian-Piero. He had not meant to say this because he did not know how it could be done but he could not think of anything else to say. "Why did you tell them that you had done the murder?" he cried.

"They wanted so much to hear that I did it. I hated to disappoint them. You know how I dislike unpleasantness."

"Harlequin, they say that they're going to hang you."

"They never said a truer word — if I live to see the day."

"Are you ill, dear Harlequin?"

"I hope so. I feel a cold coming on. I hope it goes into a consumption — a rapid one — if only to cheat the executioner."

"I'm going to tell them that you never touched the pawnbroker. They must believe me."

"You forget, Gian-Piero, what stories I've already told them. They were so persuasive. Have you ever seen the rack, Gian-Piero? It works well on the fancy. The rack can make a man say anything. They'll never believe you, Gian-Piero. Only lies are believable. The truth is past man's ability to believe."

"I know, I know," said Gian-Piero. "I never tell the truth — except now — to you. Even though Mother Matilda always thought I did. But she always believed me and someone else will if I can only find him."

"Only the rich are believable," whispered Harlequin. "And we have no rich friends."

"Yes, we do," said Gian-Piero. "At least he's rather rich. You have a rich friend."

133

"I? To tell you the truth I've never liked rich people. And they've never liked me. You can't blame them."

"The Count d'Ascanio-Lisci. Ginestra's grandfather. He's your friend."

"Ginestra's grandfather! In a pig's eye! And in any case how would you find him?"

"He's here. He's in Venice. Only a few nights ago, the evening that you were taken, he came to hear the great Vivaldi. I heard the great Vivaldi myself and I saw the count there."

"Now you are at your lies again."

Gian-Piero's eyes filled with tears and began to spill over. "I heard him. It isn't a lie. It was at a lovely palace full of young girls all playing musical instruments. And I can find it again."

Harlequin half rose on his elbow. "If you can find him before Monday noon you could save me. But you never will. So take your lies elsewhere."

"They say that the devil helps him write his music — and you're the devil's cousin. So he should help you."

"There is no devil. He has forsaken us all. We are alone."

He fell back into the straw and Gian-Piero rose to his feet, trembling. "Guard," he cried. "Guard! I am ready to go."

The guard was there with his clanking keys. He let Gian-Piero out. It was late afternoon and the sun shone in spatters of light on the flagstones. The guard was drunk, almost too drunk to stand, and while he staggered against the wall Gian-Piero, without a qualm of conscience, repossessed Domenico.

Again he began to make his way through the town. He had

only the vaguest idea where he might find the house full of young girls and his enquiries of various passersby produced hoots of laughter. There were houses full of girls everywhere people said. Down the next street — up this flight of stairs — over that bridge. But these were not the right girls. Finally he asked two nuns about the house full of girls and received accurate directions. Another fifteen minutes brought him to the place. He recognized it immediately. The moon had risen above the rooftops and the house was bathed in pale light and from its depths he could hear its music. Gian-Piero stepped to the threshold and fairly swung from the bell rope in his eagerness for a quick answer.

The door was opened by an elderly portress, a lay sister with a face like a withered onion.

"What do you want, boy?"

"I've a message for the Count d'Ascanio-Lisci. I was told I might find him here."

"You are in luck. He is here. Maestro Vivaldi has been playing for him. What is your message?"

"I must see him. I come from his — his granddaughter."

"I never heard the count had a granddaughter."

"This is a brand new granddaughter. And the message is very important."

"I do not believe you have a message. Go away."

"I can't go away. I must see the count."

"The count doesn't see strange boys. Be off."

"At least let me write a letter. Then the count may read it."

"You? *You* write a letter?"

"Lend me a pen and I shall write it. Oh, don't shut the door for the love of God!"

The old woman sighed. "They keep a pen in the anteroom. You may write but be quick about it." She brought the pen, an inkhorn and a sheet of paper and looked at Gian-Piero doubtfully as she handed them to him. She could not bring herself to invite him into the hall. Gian-Piero sat down on the still warm flight of stone steps leading to the door and, using the step above him as a desk, began to write. The moon rose above the building and helped him. The letter took quite a while to write but it was done at last and Gian-Piero thrust it into the hand of the portress. He had been so long at the letter that the old nun had dozed off, standing up like a horse in a stall, and she awoke with a start. She scanned the document skeptically but finally seemed to satisfy herself that it was a genuine letter, entitling Gian-Piero to some consideration.

"You may come in," she grunted, "but you are to come alone. Leave any friends you have outside."

"I have no friends. Take my letter to the count."

"Wait in the hall. I'll take the letter but I promise nothing."

Gian-Piero made Domenico's halter fast to the pole beside the door and stepped into the hall. It was a very pretty place, full of furniture painted with flowers and birds. Wax candles flickered in their sconces and when the door was finally thrown open and more candles were brought in Gian-Piero was nearly blinded by the sudden flare of light. He stood blinking like an owl as the Count Sigismondo d'Ascanio-Lisci strode into the hall, with the letter in his hand and followed by the redheaded priest. They were both smiling.

Here is the letter which the Count Sigismondo d'Ascanio-

Lisci received from the hands of the portress of the Hospice
of the Innocents.

Illustrious Cavalier,

*Although I am not your grandson — at least I don't
think I am — I might be. Ginestra might be your granddaughter even though she denies it. Almost anyone can
be a grandchild. It is odd how these things come to be.*

*The reason that I write even though I am probably
not your grandson and Ginestra says she is not your
granddaughter is because of the priest. He is not in truth
a priest. He is an actor, a harlequin who played the part
of a priest. It was but three days after Easter last when
we ate a fine dinner with Your Worship at the Dominican convent of Sant'Ursula and Your Worship talked
with Agostino Molino about music and the great Vivaldi. That is how I found Your Worship. Somebody
murdered the pawnbroker. Your Worship knows it
could not have been Harlequin because he was pretending to be a priest and eating dinner with you. He repents
of this, I mean of pretending to be a priest, not of the
dinner. And now they will hang Harlequin but Your
Lordship might save him. How could a poor harlequin
be an enemy of the state and murder a pawnbroker? He
would be afraid to do these things. Harlequin never
means what he says. It is all in play. But still they will
hang him if you do not help us. I have come with my
donkey, Domenico, stolen from me by Pantaloon, to
find Your Worship and I have prayed to many saints for
their help but I think you will help more than the saints.*

Perhaps they are angry that Harlequin acted the priest.
But since you are not a saint you will understand that
one cannot always go about as a harlequin. It makes
people angry and so one must sometimes pretend to be
something else. I beg Your Worship to come to the
prison with me to set free my friend, Agostino the harle-
quin, so that he shall not be hanged. I am here with my
donkey and Your Worship may ride on his back. He is a
very quiet donkey. Every word of this letter is true. I
have often told lies but none of this is a lie. If I had
made it up it would have sounded better. I implore
Your Worship's pardon for this bad letter. It is the first
I ever wrote and I had to write it by moonlight and I
borrowed the pen.

Your Lordship's most obsequious
and devoted friend,
Gian-Piero

"Well," said the count, "a most interesting letter. A schol-
arly affair altogether. A young lady called Ginestra — the
flower-o'-the-broom, a Plantagenet, I suppose — claims she
is *not* my granddaughter. My obsequious servant and devoted
friend asserts that he is probably not my grandson and the
letter seems to concern a harlequin who is *not* a priest. Altogether a most disclaiming letter." His eye fell on Gian-Piero
standing near the door and looking small.

"And did you write this letter, my child?"

"Yes, Your Worship. Oh, sir, you can save Harlequin. You
know that he is not a murderer. They racked him and he con-

fessed to the murder. But it was the rack that spoke, sir. Harlequin did no murder."

The count made a grimace and turned to the redheaded musician-priest. "Shall I see this man, Maestro Vivaldi? They say that Harlequin is the devil's cousin."

"They also say that Satan taught me my music, sir," replied the Red Priest, laughing. "And out of respect for my teacher may I say that the poor demon seems to require Your Worship's attention. One cannot blame relatives for assisting each other. One sees it every day."

"Harlequin says the devil has abandoned him," said Gian-Piero.

"The devil is commonly believed to be unreliable," said the count. "Do you find him so, Father Antonio?"

The Red Priest smiled. "Scarcely more so than most men. May the saints preserve me from those I trust, as we say. But to speak the truth the powers of the devil are much exaggerated in this country. It is *I* who write my music. Unassisted. However I would be the last fellow in the world to deprive poor relations of what they can get — either in this world or the next. The fellow is probably innocent. Otherwise he would not be in prison. He would be attending a levee — and if Your Lordship can aid him I should strongly recommend that you do so. The devil is almost certainly powerless but you, sir, are another matter."

"Then we shall go to him in the morning," said the count. He turned to the portress who was standing beside the door. "Give the boy a place to sleep for the night. See that someone attends to that donkey who is so gentle that I may wish to ride him."

On the following morning the count, his valet, and a footman set out by gondola for the prison. Gian-Piero made his way through the narrow streets on foot with Domenico, arriving at the fortress a little ahead of the others since he was able to dispense with the ceremonies of embarking and disembarking.

The governor of the prison was somewhat taken aback at the early intruders and was displeased at the Count d'Ascanio-Lisci's demand to see the prisoner Molino but he could not deny so distinguished a visitor. He grudgingly escorted the count and his party to his own quarters and Harlequin was sent for. He appeared shortly, chained hand and foot. The jailer who led him in thrust him forward to where the count was seated and Agostino fell to his knees, lifting his despairing face, already the color of death, to the count.

"Courage, my good fellow," said the count. "We have come to help you."

"As to that, sir," whispered Agostino, "if Your Worship will merely remember me it will suffice. After that I shall trouble Your Worship no further but help myself."

"We dined, I think, with the Reverend Mother Superior of the Dominican convent in Sant'Ursula a few days after Easter last."

"That we did, sir. Fish and mutton on the table and we spoke of music."

"You are well on cue," said the count. "Yes, Governor, this is the man. I should know him anywhere. And I recall the boy also. You may release him at once."

Harlequin seized the count's hand and kissed it. "God save

141

Your Worship." He turned to where Gian-Piero stood watching. "And you, Gian-Piero! I thought you were lying."

"I was," said Gian-Piero. "But it turned out to be true after all."

"It is difficult to believe," said the governor, "that Your Worship can have been dining with a harlequin. I had no notion that Your Worship took an interest in these zanies."

"I dined with a priest," replied the count. "This man is he. I cannot be mistaken in this matter. I never forget a face."

"But the man has confessed," said the governor.

"The rack will tell any story to please the accusers," said the count. "This man — this priest — not only dined with me, but he is a music lover, are you not, my man?"

"So please you," said Harlequin faintly. "We talked of the Red Priest — the great Vivaldi. Your Worship remembers it well."

"If this Harlequin disguised himself as a priest in order to impose upon Your Worship," exclaimed the governor, "he is guilty of the greater crime of blasphemy. Surely Your Worship —"

"This priest may have disguised himself as a harlequin but there is no blasphemy in that. At the moment he is disguised as a prisoner falsely accused and racked without cause. I suggest we have done with disguises."

"But he has plotted against the state. He confessed to that too."

"Well, rack him again and order him to confess that he has *not* plotted against the state. I promise you he'll do it. The man, the priest that is to say, is under my protection. Leave

142

him to me. The council shall know of it. You may leave us. I shall take charge of him."

"As you will, sir," said the governor reluctantly.

"You may leave us," repeated the count. The governor bowed and left the room.

"Now," said the count, "since I have the boy and the harlequin I think I must now look for the granddaughter. Where is she to be found? I confess to the greatest curiosity to see her."

🦁 EPILOGUE 🦁

HALFWAY down the stairs of the company's lodgings, Ginestra was crouched, crying. She had been crying on and off for three days, ever since Gian-Piero had disappeared, between meals and whenever unoccupied by other things. When asked why she cried she said that it was because the world was so wicked. Flavia tried to comfort her with the observation that what must be will be and crying over it only ruined the complexion. But Ginestra still cried and Flavia gave up, disgusted.

The wickedness of the world had never given Ginestra much concern, and in her heart she knew that she cried because the company had broken up and she had nowhere to go. She cried because she had allowed herself to become dependent on people she thought were her inferiors. She cried because she should have joined Signor Montefiore's company and left this rabble behind. She cried for Harlequin, for the image of Agostino Molino swinging from the gallows. Repeatedly it forced itself before her streaming eyes. She could not rid herself of it nor of the knowledge that she might have saved him if she had had the courage to tell her story as Gian-Piero had begged her to do. The little whey-faced convent brat had done what Ginestra had lacked the nerve for. He had gone to find the Count d'Ascanio-Lisci and left Ginestra to know herself for a coward.

As she wept she grew more desperate. Harlequin must be saved and it could not be that Ginestra would have no hand in his preservation.

There is such a thing as a last confession, she thought. She could hunt down a cleric and tell him that she had murdered the pawnbroker and plotted against the republic. Then she would pitch herself into the Grand Canal. Because it was her last confession the archbishop would be forced to believe her and he would order the executioner to unbind his victim. They would fish her out of the canal, the heroic Ginestra who had given her life to save a fellow player. The role was not a distasteful one to her. There would be a good deal of applause. A touching funeral pageant marched into her imagination. Her own body, clad in white and lying on a flower-decked bier, floated on a barge through shining waters, followed by despairing mourners and a large choir. Alas, poor Columbine! Would they lay her in consecrated ground? Suicides were not usually granted this dispensation but since she had sacrificed herself to save the life of a friend her case might be different.

Now Ginestra rose to her feet and descended the stairs to the square. The church of San Giorgio degli Schiavoni was at hand but if Ginestra was to perform so spectacular a confession she needed something more imposing to do it in than a parish church. She wiped her nose, gave a loud sniff and set off for the Piazza San Marco. By the time she reached it she was quite hungry and since it was evening and pleasantly cool, in spite of her noble resolution, she decided to delay her confession until she had eaten and refreshed herself. She had a few soldi in her stocking top and she regaled herself with pastry and ices bought from a vendor. Having eaten she grew sleepy. "I shall confess in the morning," she thought. Besides it would be much better to commit suicide by daylight. Someone was bound to rescue her against her will, preserving her from a watery grave but in no way invalidating her confession. The discrepancies in her story could be ironed out later she thought. The important thing was to get Agostino out of prison.

She made her way across the square and slipped into the cathedral. There was a comfortable spot behind the font which she had discovered for herself some time ago. She curled up there and promptly fell asleep.

She awoke just before dawn, alone in the vast cathedral. Her courage seemed to have run out. Rising stiffly from the flagstones she stretched and stepped outside. As she glanced about her, other homeless people were crawling from alleys and doorsteps. Ginestra looked about her for a bishop and not seeing one slipped back into the cathedral. Only a wrinkled sexton was puttering about but he was of no use for her purposes. In order to pass the time Ginestra began to do the stations of the cross. Midway through this rite she found herself caught up with a congregation who had come to hear early mass. Suddenly she realized that it was Monday; Monday was the day they would hang Harlequin. There was no postponing her confession. She must make it somehow and now.

The mass swept to its conclusion; Christ was made flesh; the Gloria broke like a wave amid clouds of incense. Priests and choristers streamed toward the September sunshine and there was a bishop, superb with miter and crook, at the head of the procession. He was moving rapidly away and Ginestra in the midst of an act of contrition sprang from her knees and bolted after him.

At the threshold of the cathedral the bishop and his train were caught up with the crowd awaiting the benediction. He vanished from her sight. The square was full of people. Ginestra looked up at the clock tower. In a quarter of an hour the giant figures would declare eight o'clock. And there was nobody to confess to.

Across the square and facing the cathedral the great stage of the famous company of players whose skill and elegance had made them famous throughout all Italy and as far as Paris was undergoing a morning cleanup. The Montefiore company was preparing for its evening performance. A lone figure, the company's Pedrolino, a solemn fellow all in white with a white ruffle around his neck and a rose in his hand was surveying the square. He was too far away to speak to; everyone was too far away. Nobody was near save the great bronze horses of Lysippus. They stood over her like gods, solid and still while the people flowed before her eyes like water. Ginestra clenched her fists, stamped her foot and raised her voice.

"Oh holy horses," cried Ginestra. "Hear my confession. I know Harlequin is innocent. He never brought harm to the city or to the church or to any of its people. All his life he was a player and he wore a mask and he did play the part of a priest but that was only once and he meant no disrespect. He

147

is innocent as yourselves, oh holy horses. Intercede for him and hear my prayer, oh holy horses, for the love of God!"

The sun glittered on the horses' flanks; a beggar jostled Ginestra and whined for alms. She shoved him aside with a curse and startled a cluster of pigeons pecking for food around her feet. They rose with a drumming of slate-colored wings and through their flight Ginestra saw, moving toward her across the square, Gian-Piero and, astride Domenico, Harlequin.

"Christ in majesty!" shrieked Ginestra, "You have come from the dead!"

His motley was torn, his black mask leered at the sun from atop his head. His face was prison-pale but he was laughing.

"Not from the dead. From the living, through the miraculous intervention of this donkey here. The cards proved wrong. I was not to hang after all. There is no predicting the wisdom of asses."

"You are lying," snorted Ginestra. "Rescued by a donkey! I was praying for you incessantly — " she glanced up at the horses, prancing overhead. "Why you might as well say it was the horses there."

"I am incapable of a lie," said Agostino. "Gian-Piero, tell her how I was rescued."

"My grandfather rescued you," said Gian-Piero, squinting into the sunlight.

"*Your* grandfather!" exclaimed Ginestra. "Since when did you have a grandfather?"

"I found him last night. He's as much my grandfather as yours."

"Why, you wicked little liar!"

148

"That is not a lie," said Gian-Piero with dignity. "How do you know that I wasn't found outside the city wall wrapped in a shawl because the wicked nurse had put me there so that her own boy could grow up to be the count's heir? I've as good a right to be his grandchild as you have."

"I ought to scratch your eyes out."

"Come, come, Sister Ginestra," interposed Harlequin. "There will be no scratching. We are all bidden to breakfast by the count, the most generous of gentlemen. Save your quarrel. It is music he wants, not grandchildren. And we shall have a carrot for Domenico. Our fortune is made. The count will make us members of his household. We are become The Most Worshipful Company of Players of the Count d'Ascanio-Lisci. We shall play *Harlequin and His Children* for him."

"That should please him," said Ginestra, preening. "He should be very grateful for such fine amusements."

"And we should be grateful for his distinguished patronage. However we must not think of that."

"Why not?" asked Gian-Piero.

"Because at the Feast of the Virtues there are two who can never agree."

"Who are they?" asked Ginestra.

"They are Gratitude and Benevolence. They won't sit down together. A good appetite is the best thanks. It's eight o'clock of the morning and I am alive. Give me a scudo, Ginestra, and I shall buy a peach. There is nothing like a peach in Venice on an autumn day. It gives a man a powerful hunger to escape the hangman. Domenico shall have half of it. He'll never play Alexander's charger but if he had not gone off with Pantaloon, Gian-Piero would not have come after him and I should be dangling now on the end of a rope. A great career in the theatre would be buried in a felon's grave. Let us go to the count."

"It's all very well for you and Ginestra," said Gian-Piero, "but what is to become of me? I can't act and neither can Domenico. He doesn't want to play Bucephalus. You always said you'd take us home."

Harlequin, who had been on the point of turning Domenico in the direction of the Giudecca, paused, brought the donkey round again and dismounted.

"Very true," he said. "You have no talent and I promised to take you home. What is to become of you? What can you do? You have outstayed your usefulness here."

"Poor Gian-Piero," sighed Ginestra sentimentally. "He can't do anything. Perhaps he had best go back to the Poor Clares."

"There is no future for him there," said Agostino. "A boy who can do nothing will not do it any better in a convent. But it is not altogether true that he can do nothing. He can read, he can write letters. He can steal donkeys, rescue people from prisons and tell lies. All these things he does well, so well that he is at times almost indispensable."

"In that case," said Ginestra impatiently, for she was growing hungry and the prospect of the breakfast prepared at the count's seemed to be diminishing while Agostino talked, "he had best remain with us. If he is indispensable, clearly we cannot manage without him."

"I do not wish to manage without him," said Harlequin.

"You have me," objected Ginestra. "Am I not indispensable?"

"You are a high card in a suit," said Agostino. "But Gian-Piero is one of a kind — a single card. He's the Juggler: dexterity and craft."

"Well, whatever he is," said Ginestra, "I wish you would stop worrying about it and come to breakfast. I'm starved."

"Yes, that's right," said Gian-Piero. "Go to breakfast. The count is expecting you and I've done all that I can do here."

"And where, may I ask, are you going?" asked Agostino.

"Back to Rocca. I've talked to the clock tower and they'll make the sun set in the sea for me. If I could get you out of the prison I can find my way over the hills to my own village. Domenico will hurry once he realizes he's going home. He can go very fast when he knows the stable is ahead. Mother Matilda must be missing him dreadfully and he's really very fond of her. He's shy but he has his feelings."

"But what will you tell Mother Matilda?" asked Agostino.

"Oh, I shall think of something. She loves my lies."

"You might of course tell her the truth."

"She couldn't believe that; she never has. And besides I need to stay in practice. If I start to tell the truth I might forget how to tell my lies. There are lots of things to do in Rocca. Perhaps I shall open a girls' orphanage and Father Vivaldi will come and help us to play music. I shall live in my tower and listen to music all the day long."

"So, you are forsaking me," said Harlequin. "Gian-Piero, when shall I see you again?"

"Oh, I shall find you again, never fear. Perhaps I shall

151

write down all my lies and send them to you and you can act them in a commedia. I shall come and see you do it."

"A learnèd commedia," said Harlequin. "You will write a part for me?"

"There couldn't be a play without you," said Gian-Piero. "And you too, Ginestra. You'll be playing Columbina."

"I shall miss you, Gian-Piero," said Ginestra.

"I don't expect you will — very much. You'll be too busy. But you must go to the count. He must be very hungry and you don't want to keep him waiting. Come, Domenico."

"Pierino," cried Harlequin. "No matter. Don't stay. No, stay. How shall you manage on this journey?"

"The way I managed when I wrote my letter to the count. How else?"

Harlequin grinned appreciatively, acknowledging the point. "Very well then, Gian-Piero, make your journey. But borrow a pen, my friend; let me have a word from you."

Gian-Piero looked at him for a moment and nodded. Then he took Domenico by the bridle and turned toward the Euganean Hills. The pale clown on the Montefiore stage smiled down at him as he passed. Gian-Piero looked up and waved. The clown tossed him the rose. He caught it deftly and tucked it into Domenico's bridle. He turned to wave at Ginestra and Agostino and in a moment there was nothing but a swathe of September sunlight and a flutter of birds' wings where he had been.